Thanksgiving New York Style

by
Denise Gordon

DORRANCE PUBLISHING CO., INC.
PITTSBURGH, PENNSYLVANIA 15222

This is a work of fiction. Names, characters, places, and incidents are either the product of the author's imagination or are used fictitiously, and any resemblance to actual persons, living or dead; events; or locales is entirely coincidental.

All Rights Reserved
Copyright © 2001 by Denise Gordon
No part of this book may be reproduced or transmitted
in any form or by any means, electronic or mechanical,
including photocopying, recording, or by any information
storage and retrieval system without permission in
writing from the publisher.

ISBN # 0-8059-4840-6
Printed in the United States of America

First Printing

For information or to order additional books, please write:
Dorrance Publishing Co., Inc.
643 Smithfield Street
Pittsburgh, Pennsylvania 15222
U.S.A.
1-800-788-7654
Or visit our website and online catalogue at *www.dorrancepublishing.com*

Dedicated to

Brandon Gordon,
Clara Roberts, Chuck Ford, Mary Nolley,
and a Little Girl Whom I Will Never Forget
Named Latia Gentillini;
and to Those Who Encouraged This Story.

CONTENTS

Acknowledgments vii
Introduction ix
Chapter One   New Beginnings 1
Chapter Two   Pre-jitters 2
Chapter Three   The Highway Journey 3
Chapter Four   Thanksgiving Evening 7
Chapter Five   The Next Day 15
Chapter Six   Saturday's Daytime Agenda 18
Chapter Seven   Manhattan 22
Chapter Eight   Saturday Night's Agenda .27
Chapter Nine   The Upstate Drive 29
Chapter Ten   A Daydreaming Afternoon 32
Chapter Eleven   Meeting the Goldsteins 34
Chapter Twelve   The Life of Christopher 41
Chapter Thirteen   Abuse Lives in America 43
Chapter Fourteen   The Party 47
Chapter Fifteen   The Lavish Living Quarters of the Goldsteins 49
Chapter Sixteen   The Goopoos 54
Chapter Seventeen   Dining with the Goopoos 65
Chapter Eighteen   Pre-ending 66
Chapter Nineteen   Closing 68

Acknowledgments

For their help, willing or unwilling, I should like to thank: Carol Bryant, Chuck Ford, Michelle Howard, Catina Jones, Dorothy Zia, Charee Fegan, Mr. Gill (Mayor of Mt. Vernon), Tom Porter, Sahlim Mustafa, Milo Davis, Alice Burke, Christine James, Jim Bozman, Gerard Alford (Illustrator), Amir-Hassan (Photo Designers), Geri Moore, Meryl Zollicoffer, Vanessa Zollicoffer, Irene Coleman, Arlean Womack, Karen Taylor, Robert Stokes (The Editor), Tange Carter, and God almighty who has given me the talent to write.

Introduction

I know you've read many amazing stories about the great city of New York, but not one filled with non-stopping laughs, adventure, romance and holiday cheer.

Therefore, I dare you to continue to read along and grin like a horse until the last page. My name is Denise Jones, and my son Brandon and I were invited by a friend to celebrate a Thanksgiging weekend with the people most folks call "New Yorkers." As I share this story with you, I hope you will enjoy the fun, the romantic stories, and the feeling of being in one of the world's biggest cities.

New York is an unbelievable place to be! After the first visit, most people make reservations to return.

Check this out! Do you want to know how Thanksgiving originated? Even if you don't, I'm revealing the history.
The Pilgrims left Plymouth, England, on September 20, 1620. Their destination? The New World.

When they arrived in Massachusetts in late December, just before disembarking at Plymouth Rock, they signed the Mayflower Compact.

After a prayer service, the Pilgrims began building shelter. Unfortunately, unprepared for starvation and sickness, most of them died due to the New England winter. The only things that saved the others were prayer and the Indians who lived on this land.

As a result of this, they reaped a bountiful harvest the next year. The Pilgrims also declared a celebration with their Indian friends.

Many years later, in 1789, following a proclamation issued by President George Washington, America celebrated the first day of Thanksgiving to God under its new Constitution. Now that you know the scoop, keep reading!

Over the following years, presidents followed Abraham Lincoln's way, annually declaring a national Thanksgiving Day. In 1941, Congress permanently established the last Thursday of each November as a national holiday.

Now forget about the Pilgrims and learn how we transformed this ancient beginning into a holiday of twentieth-century style. . . .

Chapter One

New Beginnings

Before this story is told, I must tell you how it all began. . . .

In March, 1996, while I was applying for a federal government job on a cold day with snow flurries falling at Fort Mead military base in Maryland, he entered the right door.

His name was Tony Barnelli, Jr. He was an attractive half-Italian and half-African-American; a hunk. As I began filling out my application in the CPO (Civilian Personnel Office), I glanced to my left and saw a good-looking GI bypass the room where I sat. Minutes later, he entered this room. I suddenly glanced over at my girlfriend Lee, who had ridden along with me on this day, and we exchanged eye signals directed to the tall, incredibly good-looking military man. As he walked over to the reception desk and requested an application, he sat down beside me to my left. Afterward, he complimented me by saying I was pretty and had a lovely smile. He also said he was there picking up an application for his nephew Jamal, who would be staying here in Maryland with him during the summer. Jamal lived in New York.

As I briefly gazed into his eyes, I was immediately attracted to this handsome hunk. For this reason, I stared at the muscles bulging beneath his short-sleeved, crisp and creased army fatigues. His boots shone like glass, and his smile compelled me to want to know more.

As our conversation became more intense, I hurriedly finalized my application. However, he puzzled me, when he stated that his daughter was home sick with a cold. Distrustful thoughts began to cloud my mind. I was wondering whether this guy was married. I later learned he had full custody of a six-year-old girl named Annabella Barnelli.

After we exchanged telephone numbers, he left the room. *Would I see him again? Oh, no, that's just a dream, but it was surely a pleasure seeing him.* On the ride back to Baltimore, I didn't give my encounter another moment's thought. But when I entered my apartment and scrolled down the Caller ID to check for messages, I read "U.S. Government." He called! Oh wow! He called within the same hour of our meeting. He liked me! Perhaps, something larger than life could develop from this.

A few weeks later, up sprang a whirlwind romance which entailed building a friendship, traveling, and spending lots of time with our children.

My little boy, Brandon Jones, is eight years old. He is a fun-loving, intelligent kid who is very inquisitive and who has leadership qualities. His favorite hobbies are putting together puzzles, building Lego's, and logging on the Internet's Nickelodeon website. He and Tony's daughter immediately bonded and always played and played until they fell fast asleep.

Annabella, who I always call Ms. Anna, is pretty and shy. She is an adorable kid who likes to constantly express herself by writing, drawing, and giving hugs and kisses. I like her a lot, because she is one of the best little people in the whole wide world. We always shared kiddie talk, without controversy.

As a young boy, Tony Barnelli grew up in Queens, New York, and various other ethnic neighborhoods. He was a typical city dweller who straddled around the streets getting into devious activities and learning what it took to survive in his concrete world. He proclaimed that he never got into any major trouble. I guess this was why he escaped becoming a statistic with a criminal record. After he reached his teen years, he started working a string of odd jobs until he decided that he wanted to "Be all that you can be." He joined the United States Army in 1985 at age twenty-four. Maybe he got tired of the hustle and bustle of the smog or the low wages associated with the heap of jobs which would reflect his future. Tony was the son of the late Tony Barnelli, Sr., a pizzeria owner in Brooklyn. Tony's father and Ms. Paulina Conner, Tony's mother, had a heated love affair during the 1960s which ended with a fireball. Ms. Conner got pregnant and delivered an eight-pound baby boy.

On Tony's dark side, his mood swings puzzled folks. He would be like a nun one minute and like a schizophrenic minutes later.

Chapter Two

Pre-jitters

Two weeks before Thanksgiving Day, Tony modestly invited me to join his family for a holiday weekend vacation in New York. I gladly accepted, because I had never spent a holiday away from my hometown of Baltimore in my entire life, even to visit a huge, conglomerate place like New York, where I had never been.

The day before the trip, while rain poured outside of my apartment, I began to pack things. It seemed as if I jammed my entire wardrobe into one suitcase. Tony had warned me to pack lightly because he had a matchbox trunk. But what's a woman to do? We love clothes, shoes, makeup, etc. Lots of it! Anyone would have thought I was about to sail the seven seas!

After Brandon and I arrived at Tony's apartment in Columbia, Maryland, we ordered a pizza for the night. We all enjoyed a thick-crusted pepperoni Papa John's pizza. It filled our empty stomachs while we camped out in front of the TV tube.

After the children were settled and fast asleep, Tony and I encamped into a romantic interlude. We held each other tight, kissed, hugged, and rolled and turned all over the sheets. The lovemaking was captivating. We moaned and groaned and fulfilled every passionate desire for one another. Everything was so hot and spicy, like a sauce in New Orleans.

Afterward, as he slept, my thoughts began to focus on the next day. It would be Thanksgiving Day, and what would be the most significant thing about it all? Personally, I thought sharing it with family, good friends, and especially the one I loved.

Chapter Three

The Highway Journey

Are you ready for an exciting journey? Well, buckle up your seat belts, sit back, relax, and enjoy this fun-filled ride of a lifetime with Brandon, Annabella, Tony, and me.

We're heading north up Interstate 95 under the dazzling blue skies in Tony's Suzuki Sidekick enjoying and exploring the many great, exciting highway scenes. It's thirty degrees and sunny, but chilly. Tony hooked a pair of CK sunglasses onto his face in order to completely block out any sun spurs during this ride. He was wearing objects of desire for a trendy New Yorker: a cotton Tommy Hilfiger polo shirt and jeans, Lugz boots, and a black First Down coat. His curly hair shone with Kemi oil. Brandon wore a blue goose down full-length coat and a pair of black Timberland boots with a blue Ralph Lauren sweater. Annabella's pink Rothschild coat was dainty and covered her blue velvet dress. She even had a pink cap to match. *What a cute combination,* I thought.

We toured through Delaware, Pennsylvania, and New Jersey, while chatting and singing along. While we drove through New Jersey, there was an awful foul smell, that of a cesspool. We all began blaming one another for the unflushed toilet aroma. Tony finally blurted, "That's the New Jersey highway smell." During this period, Tony's speeding ability matched that of a European driving along the autobahn. The children screamed as we all came close to death while almost running into a bakery truck. Fortunately, Tony hit his brakes before a major crash occurred. Whew. . . . We all breathed a sigh of relief.

As I feasted my eyes on the downtown tall buildings, I began to appreciate economics in America. We also viewed many bridges, rivers, ponds, and signs, which we discussed along the way. After many hours of pushing the gas pedal, Tony requested that we stop to grab a snack and allow the children to use the potty. After I entered the ladies' room, I searched my purse for my lipstick and realized I had left my makeup bag at Tony's apartment. How would I adjust to a dry, oatmeal face for the weekend? It was totally unappealing. I couldn't wait to arrive in New York so I could visit the nearest makeup outlet and purchase some Max Factor or Fashion Fair.

Because of the inexpensive padded acoustics of the truck, when Tony began to sing after we got back on the interstate his karoake sounds were like those of a hippopotamus roaring for food. I began to shake my head and clasp my hands onto my ears like earmuffs in order to diminish the irritating sounds. The "oohs" and "ahhs" from the kids also filled the truck. I felt entertained, but the back seat hoopla between the children became irritating after a while. Therefore I bluntly hissed at them to recollect their current disciplined attributes. This led them to become rebellious. When I asked them to sing a song, their looks of deceit and tight lips reminded me of a juvenile delinquents being interrogated by a lawyer.

Afterward, we enjoyed discussing the various vehicles which bypassed us. Especially the Fords which were sighted everywhere. I guessed it was because they offered cheap rates. I'm glad the late auto pioneer, Henry Ford, invented such an affordable piece of steel. As we chewed on a few snacks, one of the funniest cars passed us. It was a little black car. It reminded me of a bumper car at an amusement park. Suddenly, Tony sped up beside the toy figure and we glanced at a mysterious lady driver with an alien head. She looked like a fourteen-year-old kid. We laughed and laughed as we drove away from the matchbox product. I couldn't imagine any adult purchasing a tiny car like that. I wondered what would happen to the woman if a tractor-trailer hit her car. It was unimaginable. It would probably run over top of it and carry it along without any signs of damage or of the planet-Venus-looking species who owned it.

During the trip down this snarling path, the traffic was backed up on the bridge and the interstate between New Jersey and New York. We were at the last tollbooth and the traffic stood still for an hour. Meanwhile, everyone became agitated and furious with boredom. Why couldn't the highway administration develop new routes for this sort of delay? While we waited, I noticed on the driver's side a burgundy Ford Aerostar which housed a family of what appeared to be Vietnamese. I kept wondering why they stared at us with looks of anger as if backflashes of the Vietnam War, which ended in 1972, were upon their wondrous minds. Possibly they were just arriving in America and we just plain ol' fascinated them. I smiled at a little girl who was waving. She was wearing a pretty red monogrammed sweater which read in white letters MINA. On our passenger's side was an emerald-green

Jeep Wrangler with two mean looking Middle-Eastern fellows in it. The driver was wearing a squash-colored stuffed turban, which looked as if it was glued to his Iranian face. The other fellow had dark features with a pierced nose and unappealing tattoos strung down his balloon-looking arms. Both men reminded me of enemies who would, if given the challenge, try to intimidate us.

Chapter Four

Thanksgiving Evening

Whoopee! It's 3:30 p.m. and we're heading into the Bronx. The drivers are aggressive and hostile. Tony was very energetic in taking control of his destiny.

We're about ten minutes away from Carmen's house. Carmen was Tony's lovely sister with whom we would be staying a few days and having Thanksgiving dinner. We would then be staying in upper Manhattan with his other sister, Carol.

We'd finally arrived. As we drove up to the Sound View Apartments in the Bronx, we came upon many flashing lights and groups of onlookers. We couldn't get around to Carmen's entranceway due to what we later learned was a shooting. There were police, ambulances, and the media swarming everywhere–particularly around two bodies laying on a grassy field nearby. Tony decided to park at the front of the development until the chaos was over. While he gathered our luggage, I began to videotape the gruesome N.Y.P.D. Blue scene, but vivid thoughts of my late brother Lamont Jones kept creeping into my mind. This same mishap of death had occurred in my own family in a crummy neighborhood. Lamont was murdered on an inner-city street and my mother had to identify his body, which lay on the cold ground where he was found breathless. My mind became clouded and strained. This was Thanksgiving Day and people were shot and killed. Tony began inquiring and searching for clues about what had happened as we walked toward Carmen's. We were told by a freckled-faced paramedic with curly red hair that some boys were shot while playing a football game. As I glanced out of the corner of my left brown eye, crowds began to huddle and gather, as if a Martin Luther King movement was progressing. It seemed as if they were coming out of the brick walls which held them together. As my eyes roved toward the two bodies, I noticed a white chalk mark spiraled around one guy. We were told that this boy was dead and the other one was in critical condition. He had been shot in his torso, that's why he was lying flat on his face. However, the other boy was shot in his chest, and the bullet laid dormant inside of his heart, not allowing it to beat anymore. Brandon swiftly rushed to the entrance doors as if a bully on a school courtyard was chasing him. How could such a terrible act of violence occur on such a blessed day? Our spirits were diminished. Meanwhile, Tony's footsteps hurried in front of us all, trying to protect us from danger. I witnessed all the raw edges which portrayed his true manhood.

Although Mayor Giuliani had done a tremendous job in New York to decrease crime, violence could strike at any time. It's part of life. *We as human beings must teach people how to deal with it and continue to rally against folks who practice it,* I thought.

As we entered Carmen's apartment we were greeted with warm wishes of love. We all embraced one another. The folks already present were Kirk, Carmen's fiancé; her daughter Wanda; her granddaughter Neferttiti; her son Jamal; and her eldest daughter Catina, along with Catina's husband and two children. Additionally, two of Tony's aunts were there, Aunt Lula and Aunt Frances. Everyone was dressed casually, except his two aunts. They both wore 1960s dresses that resembled images of women in the mythical southern town of Mayberry.

I must now share a brief personal history about each family member. Carmen Conner, the eldest and the mother pearl, is a significant lady. Her strands of silk-gray hair electrify her ginger-brown skin. She's the one who keeps the family bonded. She's an administrator for the John Jay College on West Fifty-ninth Street. Carmen has three lovely children.

Carmen's fiancé Kirk and she are a perfect match. He's a bubbly character who demonstrates laughter when he is nearby. Kirk is a "Mr. Mom." He spends his spare time writing poetry and caring for the grandchildren. His daily chores include preparing breakfast for everyone, car-pooling for the school kids, dusting, cleaning, and cooking dinner. He also contributed his chef's expertise to this day's Thanksgiving meal.

Wanda, Ms. Diva, has a beautiful, alluring spirit. She wears New York's finest trendy fashions. She's a sales associate at Bloomingdale's downtown. Personally, I think she should have been a model. She's very pretty and charming.

Jamal, the baby, is cute and mild-mannered. He shies away from humans upon contact. He's an honor roll student in high school. His favorite subject is geography. After visiting his bedroom, I was mesmerized by the world maps which adorned each wall. Jamal has visited Baltimore for the past three summers to stay with his uncle Tony. Each time he visited my apartment, he would cleave to my computer like a wife. He also liked to sit on my terrace and gaze at the moon and the stars through the cypress trees, as if he was researching for an astronomy class. He's my homey! He will become something great one day, because he's a dreamer.

Neferttiti, Wanda's daughter, was named after the famous Egyptian queen of the Nile. She's cute and friendly. We connected right away like sheep in a pasture. She clutched onto me daily while expressing her kiddie thoughts.

Catina, the oldest, is married to Winston Jackson, a famous Harlem jazz saxophonist and a restaurant owner. They both have been blessed in their marriage and have two adorable children, named P.J. and Lil. Catina has very long black hair like Esmeralda in the animated movie *The Hunchback of Notre Dame.* She is a real estate agent. Catina Jackson sells homes to poor folks with bad credit, low paying jobs, and prayers to become new homeowners. After meeting Tony's deceased mother's two sisters, Aunts Lulu and Frances, I felt honored. Aunt Lula Johnson was a former civil rights activist and church mother. She was now eightyish and very attractive. She wore a Naomi Simms silver wig which complimented her oatmeal complexion, a blue knit dress, and a pair of Naturalizer Aerosols that were stuffed with varicose-veined legs which she covered with L'eggs support hose. In the past, she had followed the late Dr. Martin Luther King's freedom marches held in 1968 in Birmingham, Alabama, and Washington, D.C. She later married a religious man and they started their own African Methodist ministry. After her husband passed away in 1980, she became ill and gave up the deed as owner of Johnson's A.M.E. church in Brooklyn.

Aunt Frances Conner served as a nurse in the United States Army for twenty years. She never had the opportunity to marry, but she did adopt a Chinese baby named Shuna Lee. Shuna, twenty-two, was now serving as a nurse in the United States Air Force.

During the chaos outdoors, we began to unpack our luggage and relax while the family discussed the violent crime. Kirk, an eyewitness, stated that he saw it all happen right from his bedroom window. He stated that a group of boys were playing a traditional football game on the grassy field across the way, when suddenly another crowd of guys (about six to eight), ran up toward them. Cascades of bullets shot out in various directions. Immediately following this warlike mission, two of the players fell to the ground while the others ran off like cheetahs on the African veldt. Kirk assumed that all of this was gang-related. The suspects ran away.

Meanwhile, my mind felt confused and hazy. My heart was sad . . . I wondered how the parents of these boys would react after they received a message of death that day.

An hour later, our spirits began to lift as the aromas flowing from the kitchen filled the house. Also, there was plenty of laughter and good cheer among us. More guests began to arrive, drinks were served, and small chat entertained us. Among the guests was Carol Conner, John's oldest sister, and her son Marcus. Carol is a chef at a famous restaurant in Harlem. She surprised us all by bringing a scrumptious freshly baked apple pie.

Marcus, who was twenty-four years old and attended Syracuse University upstate, grabbed the pie from her hands, as she took off her wool coat and wiped the sweat off her brow. She then flopped down between Aunt Lula and me and furiously said, "They had the nerve to call me in today to serve Thanksgiving breakfast for non-cooking fools."

"What?" I replied.

"I can't believe on this special day, people would stampede into a restaurant instead of heating up their own stoves," Carol stated.

"That's not a nice thing to say. Maybe they don't want to cook two meals today," Lulu uttered.

"Listen to this, guys, one of the old folks tried to order a turkey omelet," Carol said.

"Are you serious?" I replied.

"Yes, some wrinkled, ninetyish prune demanded that we make her an omelet stuffed with stuffing and cranberry sauce," Carol shouted.

"Was her wish granted?" I asked.

Carol said, "No."

I then asked Carol if she had ever met any celebrities since she had been employed there for the last ten years. She named a few politicians, entertainers, and famous musicians. She also said that today's breakfast menu was turkey, scrambled eggs, and cranberry juice.

At 4:30 P.M., before dinner began, Aunt Lulu blessed our meal with a holy prayer. As she began to pray, I bowed my head and a strange, good feeling came over me. *We are praising the good Lord above for all his many blessings.* I smiled and thoughts began to drift back many miles away. Aunt Lula prayed like my dear, late grandmother, Gorgania James, who prayed and prayed until the day she died. I felt her presence and spirit in this room; it hovered all around us.

Before I opened my eyes, we all were standing still holding hands like members performing a seance. Unconsciously, I began to struggle to loosen my right hand from the person who diligently held it tight. The hands felt dry, scaly, and rough, like a callus on a foot which had never been soaked. *Who is it?* I wondered. After a rude shake, I awakened from the prayer. As I looked to my right to view the nearby culprit with the despicable hands, I was stunned. But, consciously this time, the hands felt buttery and firm. It was Tony. I sighed with relief from the alien-like experience.

Afterward, dinner was served buffet style. I viewed mountains of food which covered the entire table. Everything was eloquently prepared and sat waiting for teeth and dentures to chomp. There was a big, fat, juicy brown turkey, seasoned to taste and crammed with stuffing; sautéed Southern mashed potato salad; fresh greens which tasted like they were freshly picked from a garden; string beans, which slithered down my throat (with expectations of good health); a delicious, well-cooked ham; candied sweet yams; perfectly baked chicken; and lots of other trimmings.

It seemed as if everything was perfect until I asked Tony, "Would you pass me some Grey Poupon?" He could only shove me a bottle of crusty golden mustard.

We ate like Pilgrims who lacked the seventeenth-century-style wooden tables, buckled boots, wigs, pumpkin decorations, and the harvest on the grass surrounding us. With expressing thanks, we consumed our hearty meals and afterward rummaged through Carmen's clinic-like medicine cabinet that was deficient of Maalox or milk of magnesia to subdue our worrisome stomach rumbles.

Our evening entailed lots of fun! Tony convinced everyone to formulate a Soul Train line. Each person had to dance through the middle of two lines, which consisted of males on one side and females on the other. Wanda popped in a Motown CD, to everyone's delight. As the sounds Shake, shake, shake; Shake, shake; Shake your booty; Shake your booty roared through the place, the kids wanted to be the first to kick off the fun.

Neferttiti dodge down the aisle doing the "Cabbage Patch" dance. Her arms flailed high as she strode along. Next, Brandon spread his arms wide and ran down the aisle doing the "Butterfly." At the end, he simply fell to the floor and giggled aloud. Annabella decided to just run through, due to her shyness, I guessed. Carol's dance was an original and done with grace. As she held her hands above her head and stood on her tippy toes, she twirled like a ballerina. Kirk grabbed Carmen and they swung down the aisle doing the "Lindy." As they swirled and laughed, their arthritic legs kicked without pain. And finally, Marcus was the life of the party. He shouted, "You put your left foot in, you put your right foot out; you put your left foot in and you shake it all about. You do the Hokey Pokey and you turn yourself around, that's what it's all about. Hokey Pokey! We all laughed at ourselves. The Soul Train line (lacking a strobe light) suddenly dispersed and everyone ended the fun by shuffling their feet and moving their hips, doing the "Bump." Wanda ran to the CD Player and quickly popped in a song, *Do the bump, Do the bump* . . . the sounds roared out of the stereo. Tony never danced at all.

Meanwhile, the evening continued to go very well. I enjoyed everyone's company, and drinks were served once again. The spirits embellished our throats with a burning sensation that hovered inside like bacteria. Wanda and I decided to go down to the corner store to purchase our version of an evening drink. The grim-looking bar we entered was scary and unlit, like a ghost house. It had a bulletproof glass partition, which protected a Spanish-looking guy who wore a paisley printed gang-like scarf on his head and two hoop earrings clasped onto his Mickey Mouse ears. He looked like a Mexican with an attitude at the Texas border. We swiftly ordered our drinks, politely jerked the bottle from the guy, and ran out of the store as if we had robbed it. One block from home, we encountered a crowd of good-looking Latinos. I began to shy away from them because I was wearing a short, sleazy dress, which was covered by my light-green ski coat. I looked like a cartoon character or a night club dancer about to perform at a wicked club. I was simply wearing the wrong coat, because while I had hurriedly packed my clothes, my trench coat was forgotten.

Upon returning to the apartment, we poured ourselves the delicious, tasty drink called "Cask & Creme." Ooh, the milky, thick taste. After a few sips, I began to feel tipsy, and I giggled my way to pouring sweat. My rising body temperature led me to put on a half-tee and a pair of hoochie Daisy Duke shorts in thirty-degree weather.

Meanwhile, in the back of the house in Carmen's bedroom, the children exchanged views about the newest toy, a "Giga Pet." As they held onto the beeping, watch-like specimen, they fed and cradled it like a newborn baby. I wondered what business tycoon thought of this inhuman discovery. Only in America—if something is newly created, we all follow suit and buy it without thought. Also during this period, the children began playing on the floor, imitating the *Rugrats* characters. Annabella was Angelica, Brandon was Tommy, P.J. was Chuckie, and baby Lil was herself. They kept running back and forth through a sheer curtain which divided the hallway from the living room. I kept hissing at them to stop, because I heard tearing sounds from the top of the curtain rod. Oh, no, Carmen's charming hostess abilities would suddenly be forgotten if she knew this. Did these wanna-be super heroes really think this was a playground?

On the other hand, Neferttiti was our camera girl this evening. She was very thrilled to videotape each individual. She reminded me of Jackie Kennedy Onassis when she first began her new photography career.

After various conversation were exchanged, we all prepared to watch the six o'clock news. Everyone wanted to gather the facts regarding that day's catastrophic shooting. As the tall, slender journalist cast the news, his scary images reflected Norman Bates, the weird-looking character in the 1960s movie *Psycho*. He gave a brief description of the downtown traditional Macy's parade, then bleak and sketchy details of the Bronx shooting. All of this was broadcast live; therefore, as we all hovered around the Sony floor model television screen, the children screamed from a nearby window that they saw the newsman outside.

Finally, as the evening diminished, Aunts Lula and Frances announced they needed a ride home to Brooklyn. Tony accepted the request like a limousine driver and aided the two ladies downstairs hand-in-hand, like a nurse walking patients back to their rooms. Kirk decided to ride along as a companion. They drove off with two Misses Daisies.

Meanwhile, I met a few neighbors who made a yearly holiday visit to each sound-proof door in the development. All the guests began to anxiously leave because of the dark hour.

As I stepped downstairs to inhale a breath of fresh air, there stood a tall, rocky-road-faced black male blocking the exit door. I politely said, "Excuse me" and smiled. He moved like a turtle and retained his gold-toothed smile while babbling profanity under his hard-core breath. I guessed he was the apartment's bellboy, lacking a tailored, uniformed look. On the other hand, his garments reflected the hardship of a struggling male. He wore dark micehole sweats and a pair of red Converse shoes with no socks. I wished that a genie could appear to transform his impoverished appearance.

One hour later, Tony and Kirk returned from the Brooklyn drive. Kirk soundlessly approached me and stated that Aunt Lula was impressed with my well-mannered attributes. He put two thumbs up and informed me that I was Tony's prize. I couldn't imagine being his Cracker Jack prize because of his immature characteristics. As we continued to stand in the corner of the living room, Kirk's sneaky whispers puzzled Tony. His expressions were distraught and his complexion turned as red as a bee sting.

After the last group of guests departed, we discovered that the children had fallen flat asleep on the sofa from the day's fun-filled activities. I regretfully woke them in order to change their clothes into their comfortable nightware.

Later on that night, Wanda's boyfriend, Alexander Coates III, a son of a New York judge, rallied a card game. Because of my inability to play Spades, I decided to shower and relax. Afterward, Tony and I sneaked hugs and kisses like characters in *Grease* while passing each other throughout the apartment.

An hour later, I decided to lay beside the children for a brief nap. Five minutes after I drifted to sleep, I was suddenly awakened by an annoying sound flowing from the living room. I got up and walked toward that room, peeked in, and saw Tony sitting alone watching a wrestling match. I viewed two giant bleached-blond-haired men fighting and tumbling like street rats in a boxing ring. They were wearing some shiny red disco boots that resembled those worn by clowns in the Ringling Brothers Circus. As they tugged and pulled each other's necks, I whimpered and cringed as if it was a real ordeal. *How can any human enjoy this mumbo-jumbo action? What possible thrill or knowledge can a person attain from this?* I thought. *Compared to pro boxing, this amateur sport is redundant.*

Meanwhile, Tony began jumping up and chanting for a victory. The boxing match continued. As the Pillsbury doughboy figures fought, I held on to Tony like a newlywed. My mind began to suddenly drift in another dimension. I imagined that Tony and I were in the city of light, Paris, for a day. At 9:00 A.M., we strolled down the cobbled street of Place St. Sluice to a breakfast café, then we ventured off to the Bucci market to shop for souvenirs. For lunch, we dined on the terrace of La Pallet on the Rue de Seine. And last, for dinner, we ate at a bistro and sipped on a glass of sparkling red wine served with pasta and shrimp avocado.

"Denise baby, Denise baby," said Tony. "Are you awake?"

Suddenly I became alert and realized I was surrounded by the penniless gamblers who had just left the card table with agony. I was finished daydreaming and they were done with their Las Vegas and Atlantic City dreams. Next, we all decided to watch an episode of the *Benny Hill* television series, one of Kirk's favorite comedians. During this period, our tired bodies and weary eyes glared at the set, which tried to entertain us. Tony and I decided to swap the children to another sleeping area while we occupied that space. We entwined into one another's arms and kissed and then made love until I envisioned steam hovering over the entire room. We became engaged in a hot and spicy love triangle. As we moved and grooved, the passion was hot like fire and brimstone, and he enjoyed the feeling. Tony's moans were very squeamish, but he spurted out something as if he was trying to make a statement. The sheets were wrinkled and in disarray. The mattress became our third wheel. Afterward, we slept like it was bear season.

Chapter Five

The Next Day

The next morning, as snowflakes dropped, everyone woke up fatigued and exerted. Each time the phone rang repeatedly, I felt drums beating inside my head. I wanted to take a Tylenol, an Advil, an Excedrin, and an Aleve to get rid of the pain. Carmen decided to cook a hot breakfast for everyone. Meanwhile, Tony decided to go jogging. As he prepared for his departure, I glanced at his muscle-bound physique. As he put on his half tee-shirt, his button-look navel looked very attractive. He also put on a pair of jogging pants monogrammed with the word ARMY, which fit him like a sports model. He suddenly grabbed me like one of the dancers in the 1980s movie *Dirty Dancing* and kissed me goodbye. When he returned an hour later, he stated that he had run for six miles. Sweat poured from his banana skin and his hygiene smelled as if he had brought back the neighborhood's garbage. I swiftly left the bedroom, as if I had just been told by a doctor that someone had just died.

Immediately after breakfast ended, everyone gathered around the living room table like glee club members to decide what the day's activities would entail. The seniors just wanted peace and serenity. I felt they should just sit and chill.

Wanda and I decided to take the kids out shopping and for a fresh breath of New York's smoggiest air. Due to Tony's consumer-related ethics, he gave me only twenty-dollars for souvenirs after I requested some shopping money. *My gosh, we are in New York City, and how many souvenirs can a person get with twenty bucks?* I thought. I humbled my evil thoughts, cracked a smile, and accepted the low-budget recyclable paper with a spoiled-baby mentality. I could only afford to make purchase at a run-down one-dollar joint in the Bronx. After we all finished our souvenir shopping, some of the children begged to ride the screechy subway train which thundered above our heads. I carefully explained to them that this rusty adventure was not happening today. Brandon ducked like a flamingo as he tried to escape the vexing sounds of the worn-out steel train wheels. When we returned home later that afternoon, we found Carmen, Kirk, and Tony practicing a cold-weather couch potato process. They were watching the 1997 movie *Anaconda,* a slimy thriller. The television set displayed large, slippery, cold-blooded, scaly snakes devouring and torturing characters on the screen. The hissing roars frightened the children. The famous rapper and actor *Ice Cube* fought these acts of evil until the end. Tony's attitude was very snooty, and he sat and watched like a choir boy. As the snakes slithered, he watched like a military man guarding Buckingham Palace. *My gosh, we're watching a thriller, so why can't he cut out the stiff-shirt attitude,* I thought.

Afterward, Tony and Kirk decided to have a few drinks. After sipping, silliness, and boisterous laughter, they began to rise from their seats. Their beer bellies swung low from beneath the stinky, tacky tee-shirts they wore. I began to laugh to myself. Minutes later, I questioned Tony about the intoxicated effects which would ruin our evening. I couldn't handle the stagnated wino smells that spurted from between his lips. Every feeling of love I had relished for him was suddenly lost, and all I wanted him to do was check him into the Betty Ford clinic in California.

Later on that night, the family decided to play a few fun-filled board games. What impressed me about this family was its zest for competition, and the amusing, entertaining atmosphere. Carmen had a closet full of games–board games. There were Pictionary, dominos, Uno, Monopoly, Scrabble, chess, and many others. It amazed me to see how much they all enjoyed sitting around each other, playing challenging games. Carmen said that this was one of their family traditions. I couldn't believe it! There was no television or radio–just plain ol' family fun.

The final game played was an awful plot in which the entire family conspired. Wanda and I walked to the corner store and upon returning back, I decided to hide in the kitchen to see if Tony would inquire about my whereabouts. Each family member began to ponder and worry about my sudden disappearance. Wanda told the family I was still at the store. As I crammed my tiny Barbie doll figure into the corner by the refrigerator, I heard Kirk ask Tony, "Where is Denise?"

His negative reply was, "I don't know, she's a grown woman." But minutes later, he jumped up from the sofa like a contestant who had won a spelling bee, and he searched the house for me until this psychological mystery was solved. His final move was the kitchen. As he peeked into the doorway, I came from behind the refrigerator and glared at him, blushing and waiting like a chess piece. The scheme worked. I won the game. The goal of this whole ordeal was to see if he cared for me. He did. My reward from him was a french kiss.

Chapter Six

Saturday's Daytime Agenda

I had a terrible hangover Saturday morning, but I guessed it was my turn to show my guest manners. I decided to cook everyone breakfast. Maybe this would help take away my drained feeling. I cooked flaked fried eggs, well-cooked Sizzlean bacon, and toast. I made some fresh, pulpy orange juice. When I glanced outside the kitchen window, hoards of bums gathered around the window like a soup kitchen had just opened. I screamed out the window, using some ghetto ebonics language, "Hey you folks, they're serving free breakfast at the center around the corner." They all started strolling and wobbling with bags and canes toward that direction.

After breakfast, I decided to take the children outside to play at the nearby playground. As they climbed and ran around the brick-caked court, I witnessed two males fighting by one of the development's entranceways. It sounded as if they were disagreeing about some loot. I beckoned the kids to come back indoors to avoid a *New York Undercover* scene. Who knew, maybe we would have the opportunity to meet Malik Yoba and Michael Delorenzo.

The women decided to visit Catina's new home. Tony agreed to drive us over there, while he and Jamal went to shoot some basketball. Upon arriving to her house, I was astonished by the Colonial-looking exterior of the house. Before we entered, P.J. opened the door and ran outside. He introduced the children to his neighbor Dominic, who was walking across the street. Dominic was an eight-year-old Italian kid who reminded me of a child television star. The children began to play hide and seek, while the adults gathered on the front steps to discuss one of the neighbors who had left his car's motor running for an hour. Brandon held onto a sycamore tree while he counted to one hundred. He then started searching for the missing kids as if he was on a quest. He soon discovered that they were all hiding behind a rosebush down the street, because each child cried out from the sticky thorns which stuck them like they were at the clinic getting a needle.

After the horseplay ended, we entered the house. I was given a tour by Carmen. Baby Lil's bedroom set was natural oak and resembled IKEA's designs. It was surely an inspiration from the past. There were wooden features everywhere, surrounded by wicker and woven chairs and dressers. The walls were covered with Raggedy Ann wallpaper and a charcoal-brown border. Her toy chest was overstuffed with many toy delights. Lil's comforter was an old, twin-sized granny patched design which had been sewn together by a hardworking seamstress. Brandon grasped for the Minnie Mouse wooden doll which sat on the cute table beside a Disney musical clock. As I admired a black and white baby portrait of her which hung above me, Lil crawled between my legs and pointed to a ball that just rolled under the bed. Annabella got on her knees and aided her with her toy quest. Next we toured P.J.'s room, which blinded me with hoards of toys. Any child would be compelled to enjoy this playground and toyland atmosphere. In one corner stood a natural homey-oak bunk bed set with a ladder and rails attached. The set also included a matching dresser, mirror, and desk set. Brandon's excitement led him to grab many toys and camp out on the floor. There was a pool table in one corner, which I enjoyed playing myself; a Sony Play Station video game hooked up to a twenty-inch colored television; a bookshelf crammed against his baseball-printed wallpaper; and a large hunter-green toy chest shaped like a turtle and full of action figures. Oh, I forgot, he even had a pinball machine which made sounds and glowed in the dark with lots of neon lights. The printed cotton curtains which covered his windows had a baseball, bat, and glove design.

To escape the chaos, Carmen and I ventured off to the kitchen. This country kitchen reflected the Deep South. The wooden table and chairs were covered with red plaid fabrics. The white wooden cabinetry stood out against her duck-designed wallpaper. There was a pair of red frilly curtains blowing from the half-raised window. On one of the counters stood a Steuben bowl. This elegant and exquisite beauty stood for itself. Catina said she inherited the piece from her husband's late grandmother, who collected the bowls from Saks Fifth Avenue on Fifty-sixth Street. I smiled as I left the kitchen.

The contemporary styled master bedroom was a sight for sore eyes. The bedroom set was a five-piece Italian lacquer delight. A large black-framed picture of the city of New York hung on the wall above the headboard. A plush white Oriental rug framed in black covered the floor beneath the bed. Two tall, vanilla-scented white candles inside silver holders sat on both bedside tables. The scent steadily breezed through the room. There was a dark green velvet-soft recliner sitting in front of a sleek black contemporary entertainment center. It held a twenty-seven inch television set, which blared sounds from the movie *Breakfast At Tiffany's*.

After the tour, we relaxed on the five-piece burgundy sleeper sectional strung around the living room. The wallpaper was shrimp-colored with dozens of rose petals spurting all over it. Three country wooden tables accented this room. On the middle table sat a bowl of green apples all alone in a porcelain bowl. The sleeper was decorated with tapestry fabric pillows laid in every corner for comfort. I especially enjoyed the section of the sofa with a handle rocker. It was such a delight to recline and view a large gold-framed picture of Louis Armstrong blowing a trumpet. We sat around and chilled, danced, and played music from New York's hottest video channel. Music roared through the apartment as if it were a night club. Wanda jumped and started dancing like Janet Jackson as she pointed to the rappers, most of whom she knew were born and raised in this city. I was motivated by this action, so I began to move my body to the sounds. After several hours had passed, we decided to breeze through SoHo village and grab a bite to eat. As we were driving along, the radio blared sounds from Whitney Houston. As her voice cooed through Catina's 4-door Nissan Pathfinder, I bobbed my head and tapped my feet while I cast my eyes on New York's slices of social history. SoHo had dozens of cafes, creative architecture, and an upbeat atmosphere. We decided to order take-out from a fast-food restaurant, because prices in this place were sky high! As we drove away from this community, we began to see old, dilapidated housing with exteriors which had rotted and rusted from neglect. We saw emerging fashion trends and chunks of tall buildings.

It was 8:00 P.M. and we were back at Carmen's. Tony summoned the kids and me to start packing our luggage, so we could head to Carol's house in upper Manhattan. Everyone said their gloomy good-byes, as we headed through the steel-like corridor to the truck. After we all buckled our seatbelts and got ready to ride off, a dark-skinned woman with glossy lips appeared at the driver's side of the truck to say hello to Tony. She was wearing a hair weave, which was glued sideways to the top of her peanut head. Each strand was threadlike, like a mohair sweater. Her wide mouth and green-stained teeth portrayed missed dental appointments. I later learned that she was an old friend of Tony's who had been obsessed with him since childhood. She also appeared to be intoxicated, judging from the babbled slurs that came from her gravy-looking lips. Anger and insecurity powered my face, and my insides were raging with jealousy. I abruptly said to Tony, "Let's get moving at this moment." I began to wish that I had a cup of hot water, so I could wash away this woman's issues and mine too. As we attempted to drive off again, the woman's long, devil-red nails clutched onto the ledge of the truck's door as if she was falling in the pits of hell; where she belonged.

Beyond the Bronx, we began riding along to Manhattan. The night scenes were sparkling and radiant. The lights, the cool fall breeze, and the atmosphere were delectable. We were listening to the sounds of "HOT 97," New York's favorite radio station for hip-hop and R&B. The phat jams and the phat rides were moving and grooving. We bobbed our heads and rocked our bodies as if we were in the Tunnel, a hot club located in Queens "DJ Funk Master Flex" played everyone's personal favorites. One of the tunes blaring from the stereo went like this; *New York; New York!* I began to yell out the melody as if I were performing a stage audition for Broadway. I began videotaping all of the neighborhoods during this route, but the music compelled me to continue to move my slim body along into Harlem.

Chapter Seven

Manhattan

As we crossed Lennox and 125th Street a few blocks from the world-famous Apollo Theater near Carol's, we saw a few guys hanging out on the corner. Suddenly I blurted, "Wow, look what the New Yorkers are wearing."

"They're bums," Tony replied.

One guy in particular startled me. He was wearing an oversized goose down coat, large yellow boots (which were untied), a mound-shaped mold the size of a raisin, a bright orange neon sweater cap, and wild braids, which dispersed from beneath it. The braids were matted clumps due to lack of washing and combing. He reminded me of a Chia Pet trying to decorate the neighborhood. I began to sing, "Cha Cha Chia! Cha Cha Chia!"

Happily, as we drove into Harlem on 137th Street, where Carol lived, the neighborhood reflected Francis Ford Coppola's movie scenery. There were turn-of-the-century brownstones everywhere. As we entered Carol's brownstone, I was in awe of the artistic scenery. I discovered a visual statement that impressed me far beyond standard. The interior of the brownstone was filled with impeccable details. Lavish hardwood floors; Afro-centric art; modern art; antique furniture reflecting the Harlem Renaissance; and a black, stylish, spiral staircase that curled up to the upstairs level. There was a Martha Stewart-like kitchen, a large, spacious bedroom, and a huge bathroom that would fulfill moments of good hygiene.

The master bedroom was very impressive with a flair of contemporary living. There was a book and magazine case, which filled an entire side of the room; a huge walk-in closet roomy enough to accommodate a grand piano; and an orthopedic bed fit for royalty. Before the evening diminished, everyone decided to tour New York by night. Carol decided to be our tour guide. I was very impressed with the way she described each scene. Personally, I felt she should have been the president of the division of tourism. As we drove around the various areas in upper Manhattan, Carol described many thrilling scenes such as: the famous Apollo Theater; founded in 1914. It had housed such blues greats as Billie Holiday, Duke Ellington, Count Basie, Dizzy Gillespie, and Miles Davis.

Next we strolled down Fifth Avenue. We viewed Central Park and the Guggenheim Museum, which had been skillfully crafted from Frank Lloyd Wright's masterpiece of modern architecture. As we drove past the Metropolitan Museum of Art, which spanned the history of world artists, the children screamed to get out of the car and go inside to peek, but we kept driving along. We then viewed the National Academy of Design on Fifth and Eighty-ninth, the New York City Library on Fifth and Forty-second, and St. Patrick's Cathedral on Fifth and Fiftieth, the seat of the archdiocese of New York.

Beyond this, we saw the place for which all of us had anxiously awaited, Rockefeller Center. As I stared at this particular scene, thoughts of the *Today Show,* which aired daily on NBC, made me smile. Behind the Christmas decorations, we glanced down the narrow path at the famous Radio City Music Hall on Fiftieth Street, which is the home of the Rockettes.

Annabella was sitting smack between Brandon and me, and she was screaming at the sights like a battery-operated Chinese doll. We then viewed some fine stores such as Movado, Tiffany & Company, Chanel, Versace, and Gucci. Oh, I wish I had brought along my Visa, which could, as the advertisements said, be *Used anywhere and any place you'd like it to be.*

Meanwhile, the children continued to point at the bright lights and the enchanting scenes. There was a horse and buggy at the light at Broadway and Fifth Avenue which got on my nerves. The horse was fidgety and kept twirling his head toward us while blocking our view. He reminded me of a Clydesdale waiting for a parade to begin. He was tan with white spots hovering all over his tough coat.

Suddenly, we saw something drop from beneath him. "Poof," I yelled. Another chunk dropped, dead in the middle of the street. We drove off like a bat out of hell!

As we approached Times Square, there were many glizty scenes. I was letting my body thrill to the sights, sounds, and smells when suddenly we were attacked by yellow cabs. They were everywhere, dodging and jolting through traffic, cutting drivers off the road. It seemed as if the drivers were wearing stuffed turbans on their heads. As the big-headed men swirled swiftly, Tony began to do the same. It seemed as if he was enjoying the hostility of it all. I felt he was trying to win the championship for the Grand Prix.

The people were walking around in large numbers with New York faces which read, "Don't mess with me." It's true what they say about the city that never sleeps. Their facial expressions were stern and focused. No smiles, no laughter; just pushing crowds. Based on the frowns and the hard looks, people were only interested in one thing, not in being friendly.

As I glanced at Tony in the rearview mirror, tension began to simmer. He looked like a frustrated tour driver who really wanted to say to us all, "Get the hell out of my truck." The children were happy for the Broadway lights and the enormous, tall buildings. I looked for the most recent and popular play at the New Amsterdam Theater on West Forty-second Street called *The Lion King*. As we drove near the sign, the king of the jungle marquee stood high above the other theaters', waiting to enrapture our eyesight.

This entire area displayed chunks of New York's success. Oh, the excitement here, the culture, the diverse mix, and the infinite variety! It's so chaotic here and so much human drama is on display that perhaps it is better to visit this city during the day or not at all.

There were additional heavenly scenes which engrossed our spirits, such as The New York City Salisbury Hotel on 123rd and West Fifty-seventh. This hotel reminded me of a story about a friend of mine back in Baltimore named Tom Porter, who told his story about being employed by the former Ms. Duke Ella Poinsettia, a former famous Italian opera singer. Each time they visited New York, this was the place she chose to rest her pretty head. Tom also shared the fact that during their stay at this hotel, the staff provided friendly ways and catered to their every request without hesitation. Additionally he said, "We didn't want to leave that place."

Next, we viewed the Gershwin Theater on Broadway and Fifty-fifth, City Center on Fifty-fifth Street between Sixth and Seventh Avenues, The Beacon theater, and the Ford Center for the Performing Arts.

To sum up downtown Manhattan, I can graciously say that the arts and culture are divine. Also, the theaters, the music, the museums, the art galleries, the clubs, the retail stores, the neighborhoods, and the exquisite restaurants are extraordinary. Any human who tours this city will never experience boredom, only a great life!

After many hours of sightseeing, our eyes began to weaken and become heavy due to the spellbinding lights. We all felt as if we were engaged in the *Twilight Zone* or at a carnival, although we lacked cotton candy and tickets to attend these great places.

Tony's hands began to grip the steering wheel as if he was on a videogame driving machine. He began to move his body from side to side and seemed to relish all this excitement! I kept thinking foolishly that if I had some extra coins, I would feed them to Tony in order to continue sightseeing. Also, had he been related to Donald Trump or Bill Gates, we could have enjoyed an evening at the opera, devoured a fancy dinner, and checked into a four-star hotel rather than ride around and look at things.

I was slightly disappointed because we didn't get a chance to ride along the famous Grand Street, or the dime-priced Delancy Street. We didn't experience the greasy smells of China Town; or Ellis Island, where the famous Statue of Liberty sits molded into a pool of stagnate water waiting for a ferry full of starry-eyed tourists to hover near its surroundings.

The rest of the sights, which I could only glance at because of Tony's speedy driving abilities, were The Metropolitan Opera; the Russian Tea Room on West Fifty-seventh Street; and the famous Carnegie Hall, home of the world's greatest performers of chamber music, opera, pop, classical music and jazz.

Our stomachs were now griping and churning for food. It was time to find a place to eat. Carol suggested we order take-out at a great restaurant on Ninety-fifth and Broadway called the Szechwan.

As we entered the Szechwan Chinese restaurant, the children were immediately in awe of a large aquarium which sat smack in the center of the room full of huge lobsters with big claws. They came in various colors and sizes and swam around the one hundred-gallon tank like people on a crowded beach. Carol and I approached the counter and ordered everyone's Chinese food while Tony and the kids sat down nearby and relaxed and enjoyed the Asian aromas. I was intrigued by the dining room's styling attributes. I saw pastel Oriental wallpaper, padded black velvet chairs, and a pillow-soft carpet which caused me to trip every time I tried to take a step.

Meanwhile, an Asian woman gave the children a resort-type fruit dessert with a toy umbrella dangling over the top of the cup to help diminish their boredom. As she spoke and cooed at them, describing the dessert, her halitosis mingled over their table, smelling like the Bronx Zoo. My mind kept reflecting back to those huge lobsters. I began to reminisce back to one day many years before when a friend of mine, while steaming some crabs, caused a crisis condition at our home. As the crabs boiled, wiggled, and banged against the pot, they kept crawling to the top to escape from it, like slaves on a slave ship. I then imagined that on this particular day, something like this would occur in this restaurant. There was one mighty lobster—a large, black-spotted buzzard—who would crawl over top of the others and break out to attack us!

The others would then follow suit and crawl out until the entire city of New York was covered and all humans were clawed and annihilated.

"Mommy, Mommy, the food is ready," Brandon shouted. He had to shake me back to reality.

As we were driving up 137th Street to park for the night, something devastating happened. Bam! Tony's face cracked like glass as he sped up behind a big cruise-chip of a vehicle which had just struck and disconnected his driver's side mirror. Anger stole the smile which had been embedded as a clown-like facial expression before this incident occurred. Rage began boiling beneath his skin like a pot of hot water as he jumped out of the truck to flag down his enemy. As a result of this sudden attack, Brandon's eyes began to roll and his pupils enlarged as he wondered whether lightning had just struck.

I was afraid all of this would turn into rage and violence. But after minutes of waiting, it seemed that Tony and his enemy (who appeared to be about seventy-five years old), had settled and buried the problem. As soon as Tony re-entered the truck, we all sat silent like Catholics at Mass, afraid to question the vacationer who had just faced a mishap. We later learned that the man was a Christian who had just left a church service and was rushing home before midnight. Tony forgave him and they exchanged insurance information. I was glad this Mafia-like scene had ended mercifully.

Chapter Eight

Saturday Night's Agenda

After arriving back at Carol's house, we sat down at the table and Tony said grace. We held each other's hands tight as Tony began to utter blessings and thanks. His former driving tension was suddenly washed away by God's mercy.

We enjoyed various types of Chinese food, including: rice, noodles, shrimp, beef, chicken, and lots of tasty soy sauce. Our conversation was based on our latest discoveries of New York.

Afterward, we cleaned up our mess and enjoyed our fortune cookies for dessert. We took turns reading our future and discussing the *Psychic Network*. As the evening progressed, Tony and his sister began having an endearing conversation about his bitter past involving his ex-wife. It seemed as though he pondered his ten-year-old bad marriage, which ended in a hospital, a court room, and with him winning full custody of his little girl.

I suddenly drifted far away to another room to escape the horrible, gruesome tales. I could now only hear whispers from Tony, that of a sinner confessing his sins to a Catholic priest.

Meanwhile, I decided to bathe the children and dress them in their nightwear. I was pooped! I decided to enjoy a nice hot bath in Carol's luxurious, huge bathroom, which was outfitted hotel-style. She had enough tile in her linen closet to open up a bath store. Her flower-patterned shower curtain reminded me of a garden, and her decorative walls were a shimmering pink delight.

As I soaked in the tub, I began to imagine that Tony and I had just returned to New York from the military after twenty years, and we decided to celebrate by taking a Caribbean cruise to the Ivory Coast.

After unpacking, sleeping, eating, and lovemaking, we decided to go dancing one night. As we danced to some reggae sounds, he began to gaze into my eyes. Then he threw me back like Fred Astaire and swirled my body up to his muscular movements.

. . . *Knock, knock.* "Ms. Denise baby, are you all right?" Tony softly said. My daydreaming had ended.

A few hours later, Tony and I got it on! We chatted at first, but then he started kissing and rubbing my chest. I then closed my eyes and imagined that I was Josephine Baker and he was Sidney Bechet. As we made passionate love, we performed exotic sex acts. The bed shook uncontrollably. A vial of water from the Nile sat on top of Carol's bed credenza, straight from Egypt. The vile suddenly fell on top of our heads and dispersed all over our bodies. We felt like Queen Nefertiti and Ramsey in the movie, *The Ten Commandments*.

If folks saw what was going on at this moment, they would say that we broke one of the laws of Moses, "Thou shalt not _____." I'm afraid to fill in the blank.

Chapter Nine

The Upstate Drive

The morning after, I arose to the smell of a breakfast bar. I noticed that Tony had disappeared from the other side of the bed. I later learned he had gone to the archdiocese mecca of the neighborhood down the street to donate some hand-me-down clothing that did not fit his daughter any more. I thought this was very generous.

As I prepared to dress for the day, I was summoned downstairs by Carol to meet her upstairs neighbor, Rose. I decided to wear something impressive. I put on a brown wool sweater and a taupe winter silk skirt, a pair of eighteenth-century high-heeled boots, and on my chest, a butterfly pin. Last night's sinful adventure had left my hair in disarray, so I had to style my hair in a crafty braid which swung down my narrow back.

After meeting Carol's best friend Rose, I was puzzled. She was a small-framed, friendly lady who wore small, round-framed glasses. How could she be a New Yorker? She had a pleasant and cheery spirit which filled the room. A little girl named Princess, who was Rose's daughter, stood beside her giggling as she introduced her to me. They both decided to join us for breakfast. Ms. Rose and Princess nibbled on their breakfasts like squirrels. There were enough leftovers to invite the entire neighborhood. If Carol had had a dog, he would have enjoyed a scrumpious breakfast, but instead the trash enjoyed what was left.

Meanwhile, Marcus entered the house from a morning jog. As he looked at the empty table, he was suddenly crushed. He began to mutter and grumble slurs under his breath, saying he was pissed off because there was no food left. His empty stomach couldn't cope without food. I offered to cook him a bowl of Cream of Wheat, but he rejected it like an eviction notice. He finally decided to settle for a piece of fruit—an apple. As he bit into the shiny red piece of health, he grabbed his mouth and threw the apple down like trash and moaned. The apple was rotten to the core. He scrambled upstairs to wash away the undesired, corrupted pits.

Since we still had lots of time left before our departure, we all decided to take a drive to Niagara Falls. While driving through Buffalo and Erie County, fresh air, blue skies, and colorful autumn trees ruled the domain.

The historical landmarks and pretty landscapes were permanently etched into this county. We all appreciated viewing the fabulous architecture, museums, and country homes strung along the drive. Suddenly, I pointed to a beautiful apple tree which sat alone on a prairie field. I beckoned Tony to pass me the video camera, which was packed underneath the car seat. He drove closer so I could film at a better range. The apples were red as crayola crayons. Each healthy piece sat on a branch like a Christmas ornament. I wondered how it would feel to pick them and be suddenly startled by a snake, which would peek out from between the tree and start another beginning of evil.

After reaching Niagara Falls, we were astonished by the water, which fell like rain. Carol drifted a few feet to greet a couple who we later learned were her godparents from Rochester, New York, named Tazi and Minnie Goopoo. I whispered to her, "Where did that name come from?" She replied that Tazi was from South Africa. They both decided to share this enchanting tour with us. Carol had met these lovely folks during the 1980s when they lived in Harlem.

Niagara Falls is well known all over the world. There are many restaurants and hotels to enjoy. As the water sprays over the wall, it sounds like roaring thunder. We all decided to stand and view the fall from Prospect Point and watch million gallons of water per minute drain over the falls. This was pure nature and a great form of relaxation. Afterward we decided to take the mobile train which took groups of people through Niagara Reservation State Park. Everyone decided to get off at Bridal Veil Falls and watch the water spray over a cave. Brandon suddenly asked an interesting question. He said, "Where does all this water flow?" I told him that it ran into the Atlantic Ocean.

Annabella asked, "Can we drink it?" I explained to her that it would be okay, but it was not allowed. Before we left, we visited the Niagara Splash Water Park, where the kids viewed wave pools, aracades, and water rides. Tony surprised me and gave me a waterfall poster from a nearby gift shop.

The Goopoos invited us to visit their home before we all headed back home, and they would later join us for dinner that evening.

As we approached their Victorian-style home after driving back through the glorious countryside, I was mesmerized by the exterior and surroundings. There was a grove of wild flowers embedded around the front of the house, watched over by a leafy maple tree. A group of pansis encircled by bricks struck my attention. I jumped out of the car and gazed down at the flowers, which stared up at my excited face. There was also a screened porch elevated on sterling silver stilts which incorporated the roof and floor of the raised porch. Upon entering the living room, my eyes feasted on a cinnamon camelback sofa and wing chairs upholstered in a Japanese print. A red plush Oriental rug lay beneath this comfort. The rest of the rooms were filled with eighteenth-century antiques and Oriental delights.

Near the end of our tour, Marcus escaped and sat outside on the front lawn while the children ran around the back of the house to view the nearby pond. Suddenly, a small dog with a head like a floor mop lunged across the grass and attacked Marcus. Marcus grabbed the dog's curly head and tossed him over his back as he moaned and held onto his bleeding ankle. This chaos caused the neighbors and us to come outside and see what was going on. Minnie contacted the paramedics while the neighbors tried to apologize their dog's evil spell. I went around the back to check on the kids, who were fighting through a cloud of frost as they ran toward me.

After the medical technician briefly examined Marcus, they urged him to check into the hospital for a tetanus shot.

Marcus decided to be transported by them, so Carol and Tony rode along with him. The rest of us enjoyed a glass of homemade lemonade and cookies on the back porch. After Marcus returned, we all rode back in silence.

Chapter Ten

A Daydreaming Afternoon

Upon returning home, I decided to pack. My eyes rolled around Carol's room and swelled with tears. I sat down and wept like a little girl. Oh, how I would miss this domain and the pleasurable sights, the pleasing sounds, and the scented smells of the largest city in the world.

I began to daydream about starting a career there. My dream was to become a writer. I would be fascinated if I was offered a position for an upscale magazine and I would work my butt off for a promotion to columnist.

I would then consider in what piece of New York to lay my bed. My first choice would be Greenwich Village, because that cozy and cultural domain is the place to be. There were many museums and nice places to shop here, too. I could live with that. My second choice would be Harlem. Harlem's cultural past has halped it become a great place to settle. In the 1920s, the Harlem Renaissance, the Apollo Theater, and countless jazz clubs rose to stardom. I would love to be surrounded by all that history. I could also enjoy visiting such museums as Hamilton Terrace at West 141st, the Toy Museum, and the Audubon Terrace.

Most of all, everyone needs religion in their lives, and gospel roars at hoards of churches in Harlem.

After settling for a year, I would plan a daily schedule. I would awaken at 6:00 A.M. And shower for work, enjoy a breakfast, walk Brandon to school, and then rush to a nearby health club. Afterward, i would go to my great job. My eccentric office would be accented with modern art. It would have a huge glass window overlooking Central Park. It would have cherry furniture and a totally cool secretary. I would hustle each day to gather great stories to make my company become the best around town.

During my spare time, I would read, write, and live New York style. There would be no boredome–this place offered endless things to do. When it got hot, I could enjoy an amusement park adventure at Great Escape Fun Park in Lake George, take a hike through the Catskill Mountains, or just stroll downtown Manhattan viewing the skyscrapers. I could also enjoy riding the ferry through the Hudson River or the Erie Canal. My favorite delight would be to walk along the beaches along Long Island and enjoy an ice cream cone.

During the fall most people enjoy viewing the changing leaves through the countryside. They visit parks, Halloween festivals, antique shows, Lake Placid events, horse shows, and wineries.

Someone once shared a story with me many years ago about their Thanksgiving holiday camping experience in the Adirondack Mountains.

Milo Davis, a classmate of mine who attended Morgan State University, once wrote a short story which persuaded everyone in the class, including the teacher, to visit upstate New York. He and his family made their entire Thanksgiving meal outdoors. Can you imagine someone baking a turkey over top of a campfire? I couldn't, but I was astonished by that creative food challenge.

The funniest part of the story was the ending. He simply explained how in the middle of the night, while everyone slept, a bear intruded on one of the tents that held leftovers. He then devoured their scraps. Milo's dad was the first to be awakened by the gulping roars. He lit up a torch and chased off the huge, furry bear, whose stomach had bloated with gas. Milo yelled at the grizzly thief, "You forgot the Mylanta!"

The classmates laughed for weeks about this ordeal. Contrary to popular belief, Milo said their trip wasn't completely ruined, because they enjoyed researching ancient caves, climbing small mountains, horseback riding, and hiking on many trails. My mind was convinced to try this one day.

I was sitting on Carol's bed holding one of my wool sweaters to my chest as I ended my imaginative thoughts. Lately, my fantasies were taking control of my mind. *Maybe I need to see a specialist.*

I decided to bring our luggage downstairs. Everyone was huddled around the television laughing at the *I Love Lucy* show. The children jumped up, grabbed me, and begged me to take them to the store for an ice cream. Marcus was voluntarily hired for this assignment.

Chapter Eleven

Meeting the Goldsteins . . .

While several short-lived greetings were exchanged, Tony sat humbly as he read the *New York Times*. After he gazed at a few articles, his eyes began to strain as if he had been awakened by a bright light. From the looks of it, it seemed as if he had attained knowledge from a history book and not a newspaper. He passed along the disturbing recyclable product and hurriedly went to the front door to answer a light tap. It didn't sound like the children because it was too mild. Tony returned to the living room and announced that a couple was at the front door by the name of the Goldsteins. Carol hurriedly went to the door to invite them in.

Goldsteins were friends of Carol who lived a few blocks away on Striver's Row. They were both thirtyish and Caucasian.

During their visit we learned a lot about their rich and glamorous life as we sat around and enjoyed a few afternoon drinks.

After the children returned with sticky mouths and ice cream-stained coats, I summoned them to wash up and take a nap before dinner. Marcus decided to avoid this adult party and camp out in his bedroom, which was filled with the sounds of Mozart.

After the children settled, I couldn't wait to go back downstairs and chat with the interesting couple who sat in our presence. The tall brunette who sat beneath the guest room of this house was stunning. She was wearing a winter-white cashmere two-piece pant suit with a pair of Jones of New York leather boots. Her jewels were to die for. The middle finger of her right hand held a ruby surrounded by diamonds that glared as she pulled off her black leather gloves. On the left was, of course, her wedding ring. The large marquis piece glistened as it made a statement on her long finger, which was accented with a french manicure. Elizabeth Taylor's "Diamonds" perfume filled the room.

When I cam back downstairs, I joined in a toast that was about to take place. Tony passed me a fluted wine glass filled with champagne. As everyone held their glasses high, the curly-brown-haired man with the perfect mustache introduced himself as Christopher and his wife as Susan. He toasted to a great holiday and said to us all "Happy Hanukkah." *He's Jewish,* I thought.

Carol came from the kitchen with a plate of holiday appetizers and said to Susie, "Why don't you tell Denise and Tony about you guys?"

Susie smiled and said, "It's so much to tell."

"Don't be shy, Susie, this is my brother and his girlfriend," Carol replied.

"Where should I start?" Susie said.

"The beginning," Christopher interfered.

Tony placed his wine glass on the cocktail table, placed his hands behind his neck, and said, "I'd like to hear about it."

After the story was told, we all decided to take a walk around their home, which was a few blocks away.

Susie and Christopher Goldstein grew up together. They both were from rich and prominent families of Long Island, New York. They were classified as the "movers and the shakers" of this territory.

Susan Massoud Goldstein, an only child, was now a lingerie fashion designer in her personal shop in Greenwich Village. Christopher was a Wall Street stockbroker. Susie's family were the legendary Massouds, owners of Paunanok Vineyards.

Jonathan Massoud, Susie's father, was the grandson who inherited the land from many generations of prominent vineyard dwellers.

Grapevines grew everywhere. Perhaps it's the way to describe Paunanok of Long Island. The Massouds were the richest and most prominent family in this domain. They lived on a lovely million-dollar site with five hundred acres of land. Their queen-style mansion was designed in 1892. They were highly respected among folks, and they gave annual wine festivals for the town. They had hoards of friends from Italy and California in the wine-making trade. Additionally, Mr. Massoud was the president of the Monte Carlo Sport Club, a golfer, and a charity fund raiser.

Now let's talk about the Goldsteins. Helen and Stephen Goldstein, Christopher's parents, were also rich humans. They were both politicians. Stephen was the mayor and Helen was the town's comptroller. Their effect on the townspeople was valued. Stephen was also the successful owner of several loan institutions. In the past they had been blessed with three humans lives, who were now valuable Americans. The oldest, Stephen Jr., attended Yale University and was now a congressman in Rhode Island. Thomas Orlando Goldstein, the Fabian look-a-like, had a soured reputation because he was now considered an "American playboy." Although he perpetuated a moral attitude around his parents, everyone knew that he secretly changed girlfriends like a baby's diaper.

Quality time was spent with their baby Christopher. He was so adorable and well behaved. He gurgled and watched closely as his father made millions. By the age of twelve, he was able to provide his father with a family budget that would last a lifetime.

As children, Chris always had a crush on Susie, who never paid him any attention. Their families were very close and sort of neighbors, although the Goldsteins lived four miles away.

Susie always felt the Goldsteins were a bit stuffy and uppity, so she always fed them with a long-handled fork. They were also Jewish, and those men didn't appeal to her. Personally, she felt they ate too much and never looked or acted sexy.

She became a sassy and rich socialite who reckoned her life by always choosing the wrong friends. Everyone she associated with was rich, spoiled, and dangerous. They were also rebellious and disengaged from moral ethics. Susie's troubled teen life led her parents to sorrow.

Her best friend was Amanda Wilmont. The Wilmont's mansion was Susie's second home. Amanda was also a troubled teen, because her father Bill (one of Susie's family lawyers) was an alcoholic. Drinks saturated his life. Susie and Amanda watched this awful human destroy his family by stimulating fights, having bold, flirtatious affairs, and, unfortunately, losing his right to practice law. His wife Kathleen had to uphold his place in society, but she was weakened by all the embarrassing impediments acted out by her problematic husband.

After graduating from high school, Susie and Amanda became entwined in a closer relationship which ended in disaster. They hung out weekends at wild clubs and dated the roughest rich guys around the city of New York. During the week, Amanda shopped and dreamed to one day become a model. Susie had a passion for fashion. She drew images of stylish lingerie every chance she got. She also had a desire to dance, after taking what seemed like a lifetime of ballet. Whenever she wasn't in trouble, she drew in the sketch book she carried around like a purse.

She acquired her fashion abilities from her dear Aunt Lucinda, her mother's sister who lived in Singapore. Lucinda's closet was a fashion mecca. She wore the finest designer clothing: Lord and Taylor, Anne Klein, Jones of New York, Liz Claiborne, Donna Karan, and Carole Little. She also owned over one thousand pair of shoes. Susie said that she never saw her wear the same outfit from one year to the next. Lucinda visited New York once a year just to shop. She loved Bloomingdale's, Macy's, and Gucci.

On a cold, snowy evening in the year of 1983, Susie and Amanda decided to have a drink at a "Hell's Angels" type of bar.

The atmosphere was chains and leather. Most of the dwellers were bike riders. They were downright low-lifes. They poured quarts of liquor and beer down their esophagi like bottled water. Slurred speech ruled the joint, and the pool hall and exotic dancers were the highlights of the night. The worn-out and splintered wooden stage held a rock group who resembled the Rolling Stones. As Susie and Amanda sat at the bar and glanced away from the naked figure who stood before them, they enjoyed a scotch on the rocks. A muscle-bound South American-looking man sat between them and offered to buy them a fresh drink. His name was Pancho from Puerto Rico. After chatting for hours and drinking heavily, both women decided to get it on with Pancho.

As Susie described what happened next, salty tears flowed down her Maybelline-covered face. She said that Amanda was brutally raped and murdered, the first up-close death she had ever encountered.

Pancho fondled Amanda and threw his husky, foul-smelling body against her as he raped her. As Susie peered through the strands of her fallen bangs, she saw Amanda lying on a piss-stained, sheetless mattress. The little room he had invited them to had no life. There was only a bed, a small wooden chair, and a table that looked as old as Egypt. The floor was covered with a funky gray worn-out carpet that smelled like a dog pound.

Pancho drew a knife and began poking it across Amanda's creamy skin, which turned tomato red. Frightened, Susie somehow released her badly bruised wrist, which was tied to a wobbly chair, and ran out of the room to seek help.

After returning, she was devastated when her girlfriend was pronounced dead. She learned that Pancho was an escaped killer on the loose.

As Susie dried her eyes with her husband's white handkerchief, she softly said, "I don't think they ever found that murderer."

After she mourned her best friend's death in solitude for several weeks, she decided to attend Princeton University in New Jersey to study dance and theater, her second career choice. She still had a passion for lingerie fashions, so she attended a fashion design school on the weekends. Susie became vulgar and complex during her college years. She continued to stay in trouble and never had a desire to settle down.

Against all odds, she became the top designer in her fashion design class and was offered many job opportunities to enhance her career. Unfortunately, she never showed up for the interviews because she usually overslept to recover from the previous night's alcoholic binge. Sometimes, she totally forgot!

At Princeton, she was very introverted. She didn't socialize well. Her only friends were guys who were members of the fraternities or upper classmen who partied.

In 1988, her last year, she was invited to a campus frat graduation party that ended in terror. The party was held at an off-campus apartment.

Upon her arrival, she saw countless of yuppies wearing only boxer shorts and carrying around 40-ounce bottles of beer. There were only two other girls there, and they appeared to be intoxicated. They hung on one of the walls wearing provocative clothing, and they swapped different guys for a touchy-feel operation. Susie suddenly wondered whether they were part of the night's entertainment. She later learned, after the explicit show continued, that the girls had been hired to entertain the males.

Also, she witnessed a new pledge who underwent torment and mental anguish to become a frat brother.

His name was Dewey. His was the only naked body in the room. Dewey was Australian. He was born in the outback country in the mountains. His dream was to beome a world-class jockey while he studied English at the university. He was tall and blond with a pug nose which resembled Porky Pig's. He had very tiny zits on his face which blocked any signs of normal skin. Susie sat and watched him drown down two 40-ounce bottles of Coors, then he had to dip his head into a barrel of water filled with apples. He would catch apples in his mouth and drop one into each frat member's hands. After this ordeal ended, he stumbled to a seat near Susie and placed his hands over his crotch. She hurriedly found a pillow and he happily accepted it.

During this period, Susie learned that Dewey was a real charmer. He was from a family of legendary equestrian breeders and jockeys. He stuttered through a brief family history and educated Susie about every sort of horse in existence. He even invited Susie to visit his family's mansion and farm in Australia. He said that he had a horse named Clementine and he wanted Susie to meet her. Susie found Dewey totally interesting despite his rocky-road face.

Afterward, he went to slip into a pair of jeans and a Princeton tee-shirt. He then returned to join her for a drink, a concoction called a Long Island iced tea.

During this period, someone suddenly snapped a picture of them engrossed in a conversation and asked to take a second one. This time they both agreed, and Dewey slipped his hands around Susie's neck and smiled as if this was the best Kodak moment of his entire life. Afterward, he slipped a ring on her right hand. It was a gold horseshoe design. He said he had inherited it from his great-grandfather, who had it specially made many years before. He also said that whoever he fell in love with would have it. Poor Dewey. Susie looked at him and thought, *Love at first sight is an illusion.* She declined this gift and tried to give it back to Dewey, but he insisted that she take it with no strings attached. Dewey told her that from the first moment he laid his eyes on her as she entered the room, she filled his heart with passion and love. As Dewey was telling her how pretty she was, big Brut, the frat's president, interfered and summoned Dewey to finalize his initiation. Dewey grabbed the pretty manicured hand which held the ring he gave Susie, and he kissed it.

Susie said softly, "Good luck."

Dewey overheard one of the other members whisper, "I feel sorry for him, because this test is a life and death plea."

Before Dewey joined his future brothers, he whispered to Susie, "May I see you again?"

She smiled and said, "Yes."

He looked back at her and said, "I've never had a girl who took any interest in me."

Susie said she was stunned and honored. What she didn't expect was that after this moment, she would never see Dewey Clemmie alive again.

Susie decided to go outside for a breath of fresh air. She slipped the horseshoe ring off her finger and into her jacket pocket. She began to imagine living in Australia as Ms. Dewey Clemmie. She envisioned a large farm ruled by champion racehorses. Dewey would become a world class jockey, win many races, and collect thoroughbreds. She and Dewey would travel the world after his success and live in the rural area where he was born. Susie would decide to ride on Dewey's favorite horse, Clementine. This horse was a rare beauty. She was tall, with a brown, shiny coat, and she was easy to manage. Riding her was a delight. Clementine was the reason that Dewey had become one of the greatest riders in the world. After the ride, she would return Clementine to her own barn, which was especially designed by Dawson, one of Dewey's best friends. The barn sat to the left of the main one, on top of a mole hill. It was candy-apple-red with two white window frames enhancing the front. The front push door was black with apple designs strung around the frame. The interior ground was covered with lots of hay spread all over the place. Despite the smell, Susie would brush the horse's coat and feed her with glee.

Suddenly, Susie's thoughts were interrupted by a gunshot. Susie stormed back into the house and was push back by a crowd of party people running from a horrible scene. One of the guys, Drew, grabbed Susie and urged her to leave at once, because Dewey had shot himself. Susie screamed and tried to enter the house, but she was continuously pushed back by Drew, one of the frat brothers and a campus rock star. After the police and ambulance arrived, she learned that this had been enacted on a dare. Brut had demanded that Dewey play Russian Roulette with a loaded pistol. Susie couldn't understand why Dewey would agree to such a life-threatening situation, just to fit in. He had told her earlier that he never had a girlfriend, just his favorite horse, Clementine. Drew held onto Susie's left shoulder and told her that after the second shot was fired, Dewey held the gun slightly away from his head, but he died instantly after a silver bullet fired out like a space rocket into the medulla portion of his brain.

While the chaos continued, Brut disappeared. Drew told Susie that this game was never played by any of the other members, but Brut never liked Dewey Clemmie because he was such a jerk and easy to bully. Susie also learned Brut had recently started dabbling in cocaine, and this particular night he had used a large amount. Susie asked to see Dewey's face before his body was covered with a Glad garbage bag. The police agreed but urged her to move quickly. As she stood over him, tears dropped from her eyes onto the corpse and she ran away and wept. Drew drove her home. After she entered her apartment, she waltzed straight to her bar and drank until she fell into a deep sleep.

After graduation, Susie decided to visit Dewey's family estate in Australia to return the ring he had given her.

During her visit, she enjoyed the pleasure of learning about farmland in the outback. She was treated like a queen. During the entire week of her stay, she slept in Dewey's bedroom. Before her departure, she was urged by Dewey's mother to ride Clementine. Seeing this brown beauty for the first time when she arrived was just like her illusion. She was an Arabian prize. During the ride, she wished that Dewey was still alive to see that she was there for him and his favorite horse, but he was long gone to another dimension of life. She hoped that he made it to heaven, so that one day she would see him again.

Mr. Clemmie invited her to come back again and gave her one of Dewey's honorable first trophies he had received when he was fifteen years old. Susie smiled and held it tightly as she fought back tears that tried to break out of her eyes.

After she returned to New Jersey, she began a stormy relationship with Drew Archibald. Drew's father was from a rich family of oil drillers. Unfortunately, he was a no-good bastard because of his unwanted birth and his blatant disregard for ethics. Drew's mother Kelly was one of Hollywood's blonde bombshells who had risky relationships with married men. The one with Drew's father had ended with a baby in her tummy. Through Drew's entire life, he watched his mother fall into the arms of fools who abused her after sexual encounters and then left her penniless.

Chapter Twelve

The Life of Christopher

During his younger years, Christopher Goldstein was classified as a conservative preppie who resembled a college professor. He lived for designer clothing labels such as Chaps, Van Heusen, Ralph Lauren and Brooks Brothers wear. He loved sports: rugby, baseball, tennis, soccer, swimming, and especially football.

His favorite veteran football players were such greats as Johnny Unitas, Fran Tarkenton, and James Brown.

After high school, he attended Harvard University. At Harvard, he became very popular after a few years of hanging with the toughest guys. He joined many campus clubs. His favorite clubs were chess and the newspaper club. Additionally, he joined the swim club. During this period, he won many swimming championships and dates. His preppie fashions soon turned into sportswear.

He shared a dorm with Titus Jackson, a political science classmate and his best friend. They both had the same football fetish. Football was their topic of conversation morning, noon, and night. Christopher and Titus became a campus pair who never went solo.

Titus was an African-American from Charlotte, North Carolina. He came to Harvard to study law. He would in the future make his family back home very proud with his career. His favorite hobby and only personal interest was football. He convinced Christopher to join many sports clubs associated with this sport and they always attended NFL games up and down the East Coast.

Christopher began to learn and appreciate the African-American culture. He attended jazz, reggae, and hip-hop clubs. He dined at soul food restaurants, too. After all, his Jewish heritage sanctioned overeating. He became like an outside relative to Titus's family. Chris and Titus were seen during their spare time at the famous restaurant called Sylvia's in Harlem.

Here they enjoyed Southern fried chicken, baked macaroni and cheese, sweet potatoes, pork chops, collard greens, peach cobbler, baked apple pie, and lots of salty ham. Christopher gained great respect among the dwellers of Harlem and other ethnic neighborhoods. He even changed his wardrobe by purchasing leather clothing items, designer sweat suits, and basketball star sneakers.

After Titus graduated from college he didn't practice law. He decided to become the football coach for Cornell University and marry a Spanish Broadway actress named Tirzah La Viaje. They both decided to live their lives in Harlem on Striver's Row.

Christopher envied the pair and vowed to follow his best friend's footsteps one day in matrimony, but he needed a mate to make this dream come true. He was currently dating a law student from Harvard, but her brain was shallow, and despite her study of law, her savage life was not in order. One day, Christopher sadly told her that he couldn't see her anymore and began to focus on finding a job that entailed utilizing figures. He decided to become a stockbroker. He put in long hours of time selecting the best ways to mediate between buying and selling stocks on Wall Street. Christopher became very popular among other stockbrokers and was watched and envied as he made millions.

One night, when he returned to his Manhattan condominium, he picked up a special gold envelope from his mailbox and curiously rushed upstairs to open it. As he sat on his black leather sofa, he opened the glitzy paper that held his name on the front. It was an invitation to attend a celebration for Susan Massoud's new lingerie store, which had just opened in Greenwich Village. He couldn't believe what he held in his hand. The woman he admired his whole life had become a great success. He hoped she had changed her taste in men.

Chapter Thirteen

Abuse Lives in America

As Susie sat on a rock at her family's beach house estate at Martha's Vineyard, she wept. She held her hands over her blackened eye, which was badly bruised from last night's fight with Drew.

Susie closed her eyes and thought about their beginning. Drew Archibald was studying at Princeton to become a music writer. He loved to express real-life stories and transform them into songs. Although Drew was an average student, he was not making adequate grades. He also played the guitar for a rock band on the campus.

After graduation, Drew signed a contract to play for a local band in a popular club in New Jersey. He then purchased an upscale condominium and began living exquisitely. Also during this period, he and Susie started seeing each other regularly, so Susie decided to take a chance and become his live-in mate.

At first, their romance was hot and spicy. Drew showered Susie with jewelry, clothes, and money. After a few months, Susie began to witness a change. Drew started staying out all night on weekends. He would then storm in the next morning with an attitude, and he smelled like he brought the club home with him. His hangovers would last for days. In the beginning, Susie ignored his actions and designed new lingerie wear. She enjoyed drinking her favorite delight, a martini on the rocks, every chance she got.

One year later, Drew came home at 6:00 A.M. with lipstick smeared on his left cheek.

Susie approached him and asked, "What's going on?"

"What?" he mumbled through slurs.

"Where have you been all night?"

"At the club," Drew hissed.

"You have lipstick on your face and smell like you've been in a whorehouse," Susie shouted.

"Say what you want, I'm going to lay down," Drew shouted.

"I'm going to ask you once again. Where the hell have you been?"

"You are not my mother and I don't have to listen to this bull," Drew spurted.

As he stumbled toward the bedroom, Susie stood in front of him and said, "Go back where you came from, and that's hell, first class."

Suddenly, Drew raised his right hand, which had leather tassels dangling from the sleeve of his cowhide coat, and slapped Susie across the living room.

Susie held her smacked right cheek and grabbed a ceramic ginger jar to hit the drunken animal. Drew suddenly grabbed the object and slammed it across the room. As the jar hit the wall, Susie covered her ears to block the sound of the shattered glass. Drew then ran over to Susie and grabbed her, sobbing. He kept repeating that he was sorry as Susie turned her head away from his stale breath. She began to cry and he held her even tighter, repeating pleas of sorrow.

Minutes later she forgave him. Drew's repulsive behavior repeated itself for the next couple of weeks.

One incident led a neighbor to call the law. Drew had come home early one night, falling-down drunk. Each step he made required an extra challenge to make the next. As he slammed the front door with a vigorous push, Susie stood frightened by the disturbing noise. She was on the telephone talking to her mother and had to abruptly end the call due to the sudden entrance of the alcoholic. Drew approached Susie and shouted, "Who were you talking to?" Screams and shouts ensued between the two for a half an hour. Susie suddenly stormed to the bedroom door and was struck on the back of her head by Drew. As she lay on their Asian carpet, Drew wept and held her. He suddenly heard a knock at the door. It was the New Jersey City Police.

After the medics were notified and had arrived, Susie regained consciousness. She was transported to a nearby hospital and she watched Drew get taken away by the police in handcuffs.

The next day, Susie was discharged with a light head contusion. She went straight to rescue her abusive boyfriend from his jailhouse adventure.

As an apology for his bad behavior, Drew booked a seven-day Royal Caribbean Cruise for Susan and himself to enjoy Tahiti. Susie enjoyed their vacation, but she kept silent and smiled while she waited for the abusive demon to suddenly strike. She said that the most exciting part about the trip was the captain of the ship. Each day, he would wake the cruise members on the loudspeaker with a *Good Morning, Vietnam* attitude and urge folks to enjoy the many activities on the ship. As Susie told us this story, she said she used to ask herself a million times, *Is this love?* "Because I lived like Nicole Brown Simpson," she laughed.

After returning home, Drew began to withdraw and spent many hours away from home. He especially liked to hang out at the club, even when he was not playing for the band. Susie kept urging him to spend more time with her, but he ignored her. He even stopped having sex with her because his only desire was a glass bottle filled with spirits.

One night at the club, Drew was caught by another band member taking some pills in the men's bathroom. He got angry after being discovered, so he pushed the guy down on the stinky bathroom floor and stormed to a seat at the bar.

Eric Brown, the club owner, approached Drew and asked him, "What is going on?"

Drew suddenly shouted at Eric, "Mind your bald-headed business," and stormed out of the club.

Eric shouted at Drew's back, "Your career is finished here." Drew ignored the tall black figure with the bohemian shape and trotted into his red 5.0 Mustang, which he built himself and sometimes drag-raced.

As he drove home, he began to despise what he had become. For the past three months, he had been taking Valium to escape his alcoholic problems. He wanted to free himself from the bitter memories of his mother's playboy lifestyle, which led him to heavy drinking and beating on women. As he drove faster, he ran red lights and his car sped to eighty miles per hour on residential streets. He continued to think about his disturbing life as he drove along.

After he graduated from high school, his rich oil baron father paid to send him to Princeton University and gave him eight hundred thousand dollars as an apology for ruining Drew's and his mother's life.

It was two o'clock the next morning when Susie suddenly was startled from a deep sleep as she heard a door slam. As Drew appeared in the bedroom doorway, he looked angry and disgusted. He sat on the foot of the bed and glanced at Susie as if he hated her. Susie asked him what was wrong and he got up rudely and left the room. Susie decided to follow him, after she grabbed her white terrycloth robe.

Drew was standing at the bar making a scotch on the rocks. Susie walked up behind him and started rubbing his back. She then asked him again, "What's wrong, Drew?" Drew suddenly swirled around and dropped a bottle of pills, which spilled all around Susie's pink-painted toes. Susie recognized the pill type and ran to the bedroom to escape the junkie's angered face. Drew stormed behind her and hit Susie extremely hard in the right eye while pushing her onto the bed. Susie then curled up in the corner as she cursed and babbled unknown words of deceit to his undesirable face. As soon as he left the room, Susie grabbed a pair of jeans, some shoes, and her purse from the closet and left the condo. After this night, she never returned. Susie headed to her family's beach house estate in Martha's Vineyard to be alone until she decided what she would do with the rest of her troublesome life.

After two weeks of solitude and fresh air, she returned to New York and rented an apartment on Fifth Avenue overlooking Central Park West to start a new, self-enriched lifestyle. Susie began to concentrate totally on her lingerie designs. She also placed an ad at one of New York's clothing design schools for a seamstress. After several weeks of interviewing undesirable applicants she became furious. One day while she was browsing through some fancy fabrics at a downtown flea market, she met a young designer, Ms. Daphne Marcel. She hired this girl immediately! She and Daphne became an instant success. Susie's vintage exotic creations were discovered by a wealthy New York fashion designer who offered to introduce her designs at his upcoming show in Manhattan. The show and Susie's designs were unforgettable. One year later, Susie decided to please herself and her family, and she opened her own lingerie shop in Greenwich Village.

Chapter Fourteen

The Party

As a celebration for her grand lingerie discoveries in 1991, Susie's parents gave her a dinner party at the Trump Plaza Hotel in downtown Manhattan. The party held New York's most successful humans.

As Susie entered the ritzy ball room, all heads turned with respect and admiration. She wore a sequined silver couture ball gown, like the one of Princess Diana's styles, with a beaded silk handbag that swung over her shoulders. Her hair was piled into a sophisticated french roll with curly strands dangling.

Susie mingled and welcomed each guest personally. The gentlemen present were mainly old, rich men. *Is this party going to be a bore?* she thought. Everyone was dressed in the finest formal wear. Impressive tables sparkled with the finest china and candelabras enhanced each one.

As Susie completed her rounds with her guests, she glanced over at her mother, who was still a beautiful blond dame. Her wrinkles which encompassed her mouth as she smiled showed signs of aging. *Maybe she could use some plastic surgery,* Susie thought. She also wondered why her parents had invited so many eligible bachelors. Now that she was single and happy with herself, she didn't desire any of the chaps who stood around the glitzy walls eyeballing her.

Ironically, there was one fellow who held a martini (her favorite drink) in his hand, surrounded by a large crowd of folks who interested her. As she approached this life of the party she discovered that it was Ol' Boy Chris, a pet name she used during their childhood and wild teen years.

Christopher was now thirty-five years old. He was tall and distinguished, with auburn hair (at least what was left of it. His hazel-brown eyes rested on Susie's figure as she approached his group. *He's not Fabio or James Dean, but he sure is damn interesting,* she thought. Susie also wondered whether he was still crazy about her. Before he went to college, he wrote her a love letter which expressed his affection for her. He had a fetish for her that would last a lifetime. He admired her like the sun, the stars, or a newly received college degree.

After she reached the huddle, everyone dispersed as if a leprosy patient had appeared. Chris and Susie connected like a Mercedes Benz to a rich person. They disappeared from the party-poopers and decided to take a ride around downtown in Chris's private helicopter. The view was fantastic. After this night, Susie became Chris's breakfast, lunch, and dinner. He showered her daily with flowers and phone calls. Their weekends were mainly spent on Chris's yacht, which was on a dock upstate; or at an antique shop, one of his favorite hobbies. He too was currently living in an off-the-hook condominium on Fifth Avenue. Susie would often laugh because they were neighbors and they had never realized it. Chris's friends included the mayor, upscale lawyers, CEOs and the top socialites of downtown Manhattan. Also, he had acquired the best taste for life despite his sheltered ways. He loved New York and his beautiful new girlfriend. Susie wasn't completely happy with Chris, but this made her parents value her new transitional lifestyle far beyond standard.

After one year of a whirlwind romance, Chris arranged a Norwegian Cruise, and he proposed to Susie after they arrived in the south of France. After they returned to America, they had a fairy-tale wedding on the perfectly manicured lawn of the Massoud's estate.

Their honeymoon was spent in Venice. Each day Susie and Christopher rode through the canals while kissing and enjoying the appealing scenery. Venice was a romantic place. Susie was surprised that she fell madly in love with Chris in this strange land, and he made special efforts to keep the sparks igniting between them each moment.

Chapter Fifteen

The Lavish Living Quarters of the Goldsteins

The Goldsteins invited us to visit their brownstone on Striver's Row where famous people such as Eubie Blake and other prominent black notables once dwelled. As we exited Christopher's Mercedes, our nostrils were overpowered by the smells of fried chicken flowing from Londel's, the famous restaurant a few doors down the street.

    As we entered their home, I noticed the walls were adorned with valuable and priceless art. There were paintings by Picasso, Monet, Vincent van Gogh, and Norman Rockwell. There were also other fine collectibles strung around the entire place. We were suddenly greeted by a playful Yorkshire Terrier named Shapiro who had a shiny brown coat. He made the atmosphere very delightful. This elegant turn-of-the-century home, renovated and restored, was very elegantly decorated. The living room had heart-of-pine floors covered with burgundy Persian rugs. A fabulous huge built-in library stood smack against one of the walls, full of knowledge. There were high ceilings and huge spaces to enlighten the place's charm. Double-hung windows were arranged around the room in groups to provide a pleasant view from inside the place as the sun shone. Right in the middle of the room stood an antique fireplace that created a place to sit and dream. Sitting on a French table in one corner of this fascinating room was an original Faberge Olympic Game egg trimmed in fourteen-karat gold. On each side of this unique piece sat an imposing pair of French alabaster torchieres which stood forty inches high and sprayed a golden light at the top.

We entered a stunning, huge dining area with a lovely crystal chandelier purchased from Paris. It gave an air of lightness and added a charming effect to this room. Wax candles sat on a circa-1700 cherry table covered with a white tablecloth. The chairs were padded with a creamy-colored fine damask that I personally would not have allowed anyone's bottom to touch. On the walls were silhouetted oval portraits of Susie's family of many generations, painted by a German artist in the 1950s. All over the table sat crystal, china, decanters, and glasses. The flatware was engraved in gold, with the letter "D," at the handle. On a wall in the corner sat a five-gallon fish tank with a blue light, which held a South American small gray piranha. During his summer vacation the year before, Chris brought home this river fish from Venezuela. His name was "Attack." As the sharp-toothed fish sensed our smell, he swam towards the front of the tank as if he wanted a bite of our flesh. Christopher decided to feed him in our presence. When he threw a catfish in the tank, the piranha sped toward the piece of meat, biting and gulping like a maniac with his protruding lower jaw. Chris told us that a school of piranha could consume animals the size of a pig within minutes. I began to think about a few associates back in Baltimore who I would gladly like this sharp-toothed man-eater to meet.

Next we walked to the kitchen. This room was my favorite domain. The gourmet kitchen looked like an English farmhouse dwelling. There were antique wares in blue and white and pine cabinets. We walked over their French brown-tiled floors and admired the matching pine chairs, which sat around an eighteenth-century round table. There was also a hutch which held hoards of antique china. On the top of the hutch sat a wicker basket which resembled the one Moses rode in the movie *The Ten Commandments*.

I couldn't believe they even had a huge pine mirror surrounded by Anglo-Saxon platters. Most of the china was cobalt and Staffordshire.

The maid, who was in this room, offered us a cup of coffee. Carol was the only one who accepted a cup. As the black-uniformed foreign woman opened one of the pine cupboards, countless cans of coffee were displayed, as if the Goldsteins had a contract with the Brazilians. As the coffee brewed, the gourmet aroma filled the kitchen. I suddenly changed my complex mind and decided to have a cup because I couldn't resist the smell. The coffee was freshly roasted. Ms. Arneza, the maid, was a former Cuban refugee who had applied for this job a few years before, after she decided to leave Florida.

My eyes roved around the spacious kitchen as Tony stared in my face and eyeballed me about the help. As his eyes darted at the maid, I held in laughs which would cause us both to be thrown out of the house. During our first encounter with Ms. Arneza as we arrived, she had treated us all as coldly as fallen snow. Her greetings were short-lived and she made spooky faces each time she gazed at us. She was about four feet tall, with tiny doll feet, as if afflicted with dwarfism. Her mane was hideous. She had a billion dark curls molded into her scalp resembling a pot of boiling macaroni which had burned. Her face had a gruesome scar that looked like an old pirate cut. I wondered why her attitude was so unfriendly. Maybe if she called the *Jenny Jones Show,* and sent them a photo, they would pay for her as a guest for a makeover. I thought that would make those tight curls transform into spaghetti strands.

Our next excursion was to the guest rooms, which revealed an alpine personality. In one of the bedrooms, there were knotty pine walls that reflected a Daniel Boone movie. In one corner sat an old antique lamp on a wooden table, ready for a reader to enjoy. The bed was nature brought indoors. It was an old American bed crafted from tree trunks. There was a pair of willow bedside tables and a charming porcelain lamp embroidered with Chinese designs. Tony was so delighted that he sat in a chair made out of tree bark, with branches as the armrests. "Brawny would love this room, don't you think?"

The second room was a European delight. The cherry bed was enhanced by a luxurious royal lace fabric blanket. The magnificent red wool drapes gave the room a comfortable atmosphere. On the side of the bed stood a small oval rosewood table with an antique clock. On one wall hung a European oil painting of a brunette woman descending from a cherry tree, holding a bouquet of roses. Her bare feet were in a lily pond surrounded with petals, which flowed around them. She was wearing a French taffeta gown which revealed her creamy skin. After a few glances, I felt she resembled an angel who would make someone's dreams come true.

Another guest bedroom had a spacious ambiance. The bedroom set was designed by a European decorator. Directly in front of her French armoire with gold fringes stood an unexpected wooden coffee table. This table was donned in pink and white chintz, jagged-edge lace, and linen. There was a tablecloth draped down the sides with appreciation. The mahogany wooden bedpost stood up with a sheer, crisp, mesh fabric that swung over top to block the sun rays cascading through the large oval windows. There was a Thomasville sturdy recliner chair, which stood on four wooden legs. It was red velvet, designed with an Oriental print rug across which it was a pleasure to walk. A striking oil painting of an old man sitting at a baby grand piano was very interesting. The portrait was of old Granddad Massoud, who had started the well-known Indian winery estate of which Susie was now part. Over the bed stood a steel candelabra in which a beeswax scented candle burned, bringing a sense of relaxation to the room. In the corner by the bedroom door stood a palm tree with leaves spread high above the top of the hinge. On one of the walls was a beautiful, gold, curvy shelf supported by corbels and full of antique pieces. A sterling silver vase full of fresh white roses and a silver antique pair of candlesticks were among the treasures displayed.

The master bedroom was designed in a Mediterranean style. It orchestrated light and space. There was a big window which energized every inch of its domain. The sun shimmered across the white ceramic tile floors and walls and cut through the clear glass, chrome, and stainless steel fixtures of the bathroom. The tile walls had diamond-pattern border tiles and cross-shaped chrome faucet handles. I was fascinated with the whirlpool tub which sat under the window. There was also a stainless steel washbasin that floated in a glossy "pool" of clear glass. On the mirrored shower door were gold handles that opened to a green tiled wall with sprouting green trees and shrubs, resembling a rain forest. It was such a soothing and inspirational atmosphere.

Once the tour was over, we all sat around and began chatting about religion and politics. Both topics led to heated arguments amongst individuals. Susie was a Roman Catholic and Christopher a Jew. Chris stated that he worshipped only God and not His son Jesus. He also said he lived for his two favorite times of the year, Rosh Hashanah and Hanukkah. Susie seemed subdued by the words that spurted from between his Jewish lips as she held onto a stunning set of pearls that hung from her neck. Susie said she had warned Chris that he needed to change his religious beliefs, because they were complex. *How could she say this to her husband?* I thought. *After all, they are both married now.* Chris suddenly screeched, "Well Susie, why don't you change your religious chant, 'Oh, Mother Mary of God'?"

"Don't start you schmuck," Susie shouted.

I decided to intervene and enlighten them both with my beliefs. First I asked them both, "Do you guys believe that Jesus Christ once walked on the earth and is our savior?"

"No," Christopher replied. Susie hunched her fragile shoulders.

I then gave them a brief history of my religion, and they sat silent as lambs until I was finished preaching the word. I simply implied that each person who is born must accept Jesus Christ as a personal savior, confess those beliefs, and then live accordingly to the Holy Bible.

Christopher suddenly rose up and opened a cherry box filled with Royal Jamaican Churchill cigars. He quickly lit one and puffed without shame or respect for his guests. He then abruptly left the room. After he returned a few minutes later, he said, "I don't think that I can ever accept him."

I glanced over at Christopher and felt pain and sadness. *He will one day be lost,* I thought.

"Let's talk about politics now," Susie abruptly shouted.

"Gladly," Carol mumbled.

I urged Christopher to loosen up and research a possible transition in the future. Susie asked everyone how they felt about a woman being the president of the United States in the future.

"It will never happen," Christopher blabbered.

"Why?" Susie replied.

"They're too emotional, and P.M.S. may strike at any moment," Chris shouted.

"I think they could give our country some color, stability, and a new outlook on honor," Susie said.

"They're only needed for one thing," Chris said.

"Excuse me," Carol interrupted.

Susie stood up, put her hands on her waist, and swiftly left the room. Controversy continued to swirl among us. Tony laughed like a comedian and sipped on his mug filled with Heineken beer. I told Christopher his views on women and religion were both biased, and he needed to search himself.

"Who made you an expert?" he suddenly uttered.

Susie returned with a glass of chardonnay wine and told Chris she would deal with him later. Suddenly, the conversation ended with a stormy marital brew. They both started feuding.

After the fire ignited and Chris's face turned red as the devil himself, he tossed his hands high in the air and tried to connect with the spirit to agree with him. Susie rolled her sky-blue eyes at him and said, "Let's end this whole conversation."

Chris pointed his long finger at her as if he was holding a laser gun and said, "Be my guest."

Chapter Sixteen

The Goopoos

We all stood up and thanked the furious couple for a delightful dilemma and hastily left the devil-filled atmosphere.

It was time to prepare dinner, because Carol had invited her godparents, the Goopoos, to join us. Carol had already prepared a turkey and ham a few days before, so all we had to cook were some trimmings. We made some festive meatballs from a mixture of pepperoni, sausage, celery, chopped parsley, and garlic powder; a large bowl of sausage cornbread stuffing; roast pork with green peppers and onions served over top of some mashed potatoes; and a pea soup garnished with chives and ground black pepper. For the children, Carol whipped up a few cheese balls made out of ground turkey.

Meeting the Goopoos earlier had been memorable. They were earthy folks. Carol's godmother Minnie was a vibrant older lady who laughed like Phyllis Diller. She was a short, cinnamon-skinned, gray-haired, round-shaped woman who could have stood to lose a few pounds. It was difficult for her to move quickly because she weighed over two hundred pounds, but she was a glamorous sight. She wore the finest handmade Afro-centric clothes and bone-type African jewelry. Her shoes were cute one-half inch heels, but her feet rose out of them like baking yeast bread.

Mr. Tazi Goopoo was a slim-built, mousy figure. He wore black wire-framed glasses resembling Woody Allen's. His skin was dark as roof tar. He was a very nice man with a firm face.

While the aroma of dinner continued to breeze throughout the house, Perrier water and Bacardi Breezers were shared in delight. Marcus decided to take the kids to an afternoon movie until dinner time.

Mrs. Goopoo said that she wanted to share her and her husband's romantic love story with us until the food was ready. At the end of it, I was filled with tears of joy and hopes for something great to happen in my life.

In 1975, Minnie and Tazi met at JFK Airport while trying to flag down a taxi from the terminal. Fortunately, due to the large crowds of travelers, they enjoyed a quick conversation about why they had both decided to come to this big city. Tazi decided to go first because his story was so detailed.

Tazi was born in South Africa in a country called Botswana. The first South Africans were the San and the Khaisan. From about AD. 300, and for many centuries after, Banti-speaking people such as the Zulu, Xhosa, and Sesotho moved into this region.

Many years later, 3 Europeans were joining Dutch farmers in seizing land. The later 1800s saw a series of bitter territorial wars between the British, the Boers, and Tazi's forefathers, the Zeilus.

By the end of the 1800s, all black South Africans had lost their independence. Throughout the 1900s, South African policies were dominated by a minority white government ruled by apartheid.

For these reasons, Tazi and his family suffered discrepancies of self-independence while living in their own domain.

Minnie was a Southern belle. She was raised in Atlanta, Georgia. At the age of ten, she cried to visit galleries and museums. She also worked magic with her hands. She began enjoying sculpting historical figures as a hobby and had dreams to one day become an artist.

Unfortunately, she and her family were dirt poor, so she hardly had funds to purchase art supplies.

For years, she was saddened by her family's penniless woes, so she decided to work at one of the town's museums to admire other artists' talents. Most of the positions available were for tour guide attendants, janitorial help, or gift shop clerks. She decided to take the training course for conducting tours. She didn't have the spark to keep the trailing museum visitors interested, but she never gave up her dream. Sometimes, she would bring some of her own sculptures to work to show her talents, but they didn't seem to get her anywhere. She then became very depressed and started overeating. Eating, rather than art, became her hobby. Her favorite snacks were ice cream, deli sandwiches, cookies, candy, soda pops, and greasy potato chips. Each day after work, she would purchase these items and sneak them into her bedroom as if she were seeing a man. She would then devour all of it until her stomach roared.

The year before she came to New York, she was offered another job at a nearby art gallery. Here she became very popular among the scheduled museum artists and buyers. During one of the open house displays, she decided to bring some of her own pieces and sneak them into a glass showcase without anyone's approval.

Delray Jackson, her furious, egotistical boss, learned of her obscured deceitful masquerade and summoned her to his office immediately.

Instead of facing the music, she gathered up her belongings and told her best friend, Michelle Lester, that she would never return. Later that night, Michelle called her and said one of the buyers was interested in one of her pieces. Minnie jumped for joy and kissed the mouthpiece of the phone that stood between her and her friend. Michelle also said that Mr. Jackson commanded that she return to work or she would be terminated. Minnie told Michelle to give Mr. Jackson a message that no one commanded her but God Almighty. A few weeks later after she made her first sale, she set off to New York to follow her dreams.

After maybe an hour's wait, a taxi became available. Both Tazi and Minnie exchanged telephone numbers and ventured off to their expectations of a great life in the "Big Apple."

After several years of storms, hail, and rain in their lives, they still found love and happiness after their life together began.

Minnie took her small savings and rented a small room in the Bronx. She then took a job as a barmaid at a nearby liquor joint. A week later, Tazi called and asked to see her again. They met downtown on Broadway and enjoyed a nice dinner at an Italian spot. They relaxed and got to know one another. Afterward, they both enjoyed a late night movie and later took the train home in separate directions.

Tazi was staying at the YMCA in Queens until he found work and a home. Every weekend, the couple met at various places around town and became closer and closer.

Six weeks passed, and Minnie decided to invite him over to her place for a drink. After maybe and hour, they embraced into a love triangle which led to a hot and steamy night of passion and history.

The next day, Tazi started driving for a taxi service and Minnie suggested that he become her roommate until he could find proper living quarters. "Did he think that he would get away from me now?" Minnie said as she smiled.

A few weeks later, Tazi saved up enough money to buy Minnie a ring, and he proposed to her in the middle of Madison Square Garden on a lovely spring day. Afterward, they ventured off to Central Park and rode around it on a horse and buggy as a celebration.

Their weekend honeymoon was spent on Staten Island at South Shore, a trip paid for by Minnie's best friend, Michelle. On the Monday following their return, they began to search for a place to start their new life. Because their funds were low, the poverty definition ruled their search. They looked at apartments in the Bronx and Harlem without any success. They finally settled for an affordable second-floor loft in Brooklyn. The neighborhood they selected was totally gruesome. Their neighbors were mainly Puerto-Rican families, junkies, and alcoholics who dressed the corners of the streets, and prostitutes who sashayed up and down the concrete twenty-four hours a day. Their apartment sat over a bar that catered to the lowest of human slime who drank there.

Tazi soon found a job working for a janitorial service waxing and buffing floors, while Minnie found work at a factory which produced paper. With the pennies they both earned, they were able to fill their home with second-hand furniture purchased at surrounding thrift shops. The plumbing in the place was so inadequate they had to heat water all the time to wash up. The landlord was an old haggard, Jewish woman named Sarah who never offered to fix or repair a thing! The worst part about the place were the roaches and rodents who ruled the house. They crawled around and patiently waited for any sign of something to eat. Tazi shouted, "I don't know how they survive, because our meals consist mainly of canned foods, which leave no scraps." Whenever Tazi was able to work overtime, he treated Minnie to a pizza or bought a piece of steak at the grocery store.

In 1978, Minnie began to feel fatigued and had excruciating pains in her stomach. One night as she showered, she screamed in a high pitch, "Tazi come in here."

As he dropped his pen on the kitchen table where he was writing a letter to his brother in Africa, he ran to the forward cries. Once he arrived, he found Minnie standing in the shower crying while water poured over her head. She explained to him through sobs that she felt sharp pains in the lower part of her tummy. He helped Minnie out of the tub and dried her off while he held her.

The next day, after an emergency hospital visit, Minnie was diagnosed with stomach cancer. She was referred to an oncologist, who recommended that she have a hysterectomy in order to survive this mean disease. Minnie agreed to the surgical process, but bitterness gloomed her spirits. She was unable to work during her treatments and found herself falling into a deep depression.

During this time, Tazi had to work other menial jobs to make ends meet. Therefore, he was not always there for Minnie's emotional support during her illness. Her family frequently visited and assisted with funds for her medicine. Her best friend Michelle stayed for a week after the surgery, and she helped Minnie recover a little.

After months of treatment and pill-popping, Minnie's cancer totally vanished. Despite her misfortune of a life without any hope for children in the future, she replaced her worries with poor eating habits. She began to overindulge in anything her mouth could consume.

One day Tazi decided to visit St. Patrick's Cathedral to pray. He pleaded as he lit several candles and fell toward an ivory statue which stared at him with a frozen eye. He contemplated his life as a husband. He had waddled through a string of jobs ranging from a janitor to a prison guard. He truly wanted to make a better life for his wife and himself. Additionally, he wanted Minnie to have good health.

After the prayer, he straddled out of the vestibule with glaring eyes and an idea. The next day, he registered for classes at the New York City College on 135th and Convent Streets. Here he studied education and graduated a few years later with a BA degree in history and advanced education. During the years he studied, he decided to indulge in African-American studies. With this career, he could educate others as well as himself about our advances to freedom. He was fascinated with the many Africans who took the challenge to come to America to prosper on their own, without being brought over on a wooden boat governed by slave traders. He despised those men who split up African families and brought them over to a strange country without their permission. Before he went to bed at night, he prayed to overcome the secret racial barriers that would stagnate his future. His favorite escape was to listen to the late Dr. Martin Luther King's speeches on cassette. As Dr. King orated, "Black men and white men will one day join hands together," Tazi would relax and smile in meditative delight. If he could let go of his African pride and prejudices, he could live in peace and harmony with all men.

Tazi's new career at the New York City College as an African-American history professor was very interesting and challenging. Each semester he would enlighten his new students with stories of his hardships and struggles in South Africa. He also taught the students about the African-American history which led us all to freedom. The topics were African Culture, Slave Trade in the New World, Negroes in the Colonial Era, The Turn of the Century, Negro Pioneers in the Westward March, The Civil War, Philanthropy, Racial Issues, The Harlem Renaissance, and Progress in Our Current Urban America. At the end of each semester, in order to pass the class, each student was required to present one of these topics in an artistic way. They had three options for their presentation: pictures, art forms, or an acting demonstration.

Tazi would never forget one student of his. His name was Dranoto Williams, a black male student from the Bronx. Dranoto presented a Booker T. Washington speech which brought tears to Tazi's eyes. Mr. Williams recited one of Mr. Washingtons's speeches and strongly spoke out to the class on labor-force issues and education for blacks. The funniest part of the presentation was his attire. He wore an 1800s black suit and a distinguished polka-dot bow tie that reflected the fashion history of that era. After his speech came to an end, the word spread all over the campus about his performance. Dranoto Williams later was elected to act out his presentation at various schools, museums, and functions all around New York City.

In 1980, the Goopoos were able to move to Harlem in a brownstone on 137th Street. The house needed to be restored and repaired, but

Minnie was thrilled with the idea of this new project. During this period of their marriage, Tazi spent long hours away from home. In addition to many other educational tasks, he prepared lessons for his students, wrote theses, and arranged field trips to museums all over America such as the Walter Art Gallery in Maryland and the Smithsonian in Washington D.C.

Minnie became close friends with her next-door neighbor, Carol. They both spent a lot of time rummaging through their favorite American flea market on Twenty-sixth Street and Santa Fe, going to Broadway plays, decorating their brownstones, and enjoying a cup of tea with gossip. Carol found the best neighbors she'd ever had. Any time she faced problems or needed motherly advice, Minnie was always there for support. When Carol had dates, Minnie even gladly offered to watch Marcus, who was six years old. He enjoyed visiting the Goopoos because they had one of IBM's first computers, and he liked to play with it. The computer had many educational and fun-filled games. Marcus would spend hours poking on the keyboard, although he wasn't computer-literate. Tazi would take time and teach him the basics. One night during the Christmas holiday, Carol wanted to surprise the Goopoos with a gift to show her appreciation of their friendship. She had spent many hours sewing and crocheting an afghan blanket covered with assorted colors. As she presented this warm and cozy gift, the Goopoos asked her to become their godchild. Carol felt pleased and happy.

After her decorating process ended, Minnie was pleased with the results. In one of her spare rooms, she had decided to set up an area to sculpt. In this room was a large steel conference table in front of a round window. It was a spot for relaxation and reflection on the outside beauty. She was feeling better these days, so she had new creative ideas in mind. She would awaken each day by the crack of dawn and work until sunset. She began to carve and sculpt African images and designs of wood, stone, and ivory. Her work was original and defined. She was urged by a friend named Kitten to sell her pieces at a local flea market. To her gleeful surprise, her pieces sold like food! As soon as someone viewed the lovely art, a purchase was immediately made. As quickly as she designed her artworks, they were sold by eye contact. A business associate of hers urged her to invest in opening a gallery or museum. Two years later, after she took a few business courses, she took his advice and opened up an African museum called Goopoo's African Art Gallery. On opening night, she invited many prominent museum owners and dwellers to share her dazzling show of art. Her designs brought awe and admiration from many people. She sold many sculptures and was gladly received by the best artists as a future success. Sarah Humes, an outstanding painter, became one of her best friends. Her works were hung in the American Academy and Institute of Arts. She had graduated from Fisk University. Sarah's late grandmother received many years of recognition for her black and white drawings during the Harlem Renaissance. Being friends with Sarah led to a higher level in the art world.

Knowing these folks enhanced her reputation and helped her work become increasingly sought. Minnie became tickled pink one day when one of her ivory sculptures was selected to become a permanent display at the Studio Museum on West 125th Street.

In 1981, on their fifth anniversary, Minnie decided to have a special dinner party for her husband at her art gallery. The night promised the appearance of all their friends and family, and they all enjoyed a buffet dinner. They also got a chance to view the latest artworks Minnie had designed. The buffet table held gourmet delights such as grilled Cajun turkey, corned beef, sliced pork tenderloin, pasta, chicken salad, honey-roasted turkey, and shrimp salad. Minnie snickered and held her hands over her mouth as she mumbled that a whole bowl of steamed shrimp had vanished from the table. It was later discovered that Minnie's obese brother Paul had been caught in the backroom storage room finishing up the seafood delight. Minnie and Tazi laughed as they said he was always known as "Mike" during his childhood years because he ate up everybody's leftovers.

The main event of the evening was when Minnie presented a special gift to her husband. As the ivory figure rolled out on the floor, everyone stood still like statues and watched in amazement. Minnie had designed an ivory book figure with a glass table top which stood on fourteen karat gold wheels for Tazi's use in his writing career. Tazi's eyes popped open wide like Buckwheat's as he grabbed his wife around the neck and waist. He then gave her a big kiss on her cheek with appreciation. It was an unforgettable piece of work!

In 1982, during the summer break, Tazi decided to write a book. He was tired of telling his African story. He wanted to write and share it with the world.

Tazi and his older brother Pierre were raised by their grandparents on a farm in Botswana. In 1961, their parents were murdered during one of the apartheid riots and massacres in South Africa. They both attended rallies and political parties because they were members of a freedom group called the Zulus. On the farm, Tazi and Pierre learned to graze sheep and cattle. They also raised chickens and other fowl. Tazi's grandfather's farm was also known as the social universe of Botswana, because he enlightened folks with African songs and tales of his forefathers who were once slaves. In Africa, few languages were reduced to writing, but Tazi met a chief of the Yoroba tribe named Pa-Sadi who taught him how to read and write. Pa-Sadi was thrilled by Tazi's grandfather's entertaining talents, so he became a regular visitor of the farm. After Tazi learned to write, he wrote many short stories about his parents and forefathers who were slaves. Much later, one of Tazi's stories was selected by the University of Zimbabwe to be placed in its history books. He was also rewarded a large sum of Pula currency from his country for his place in history.

Tazi's story was about the difficulty with which the Christian religion was accepted in South Africa, because people believed the practice interfered with families and homes. People in this part of the country were members of tribal worship and reluctant to accepting a new religion. Tazi's story became popular in cities like Johannesburg, and many people transformed their lives and changed to worship with the Christians. Tazi's dream was to come to America and one day become an African storyteller and writer.

Well after his stories began to sell in his country in 1974, he finally decided to use the funds that he had acquired to go to America. He chose the city of New York because he was told that this city was economically the place to be!

Prosperity engulfed the Goopoos life now. In 1983, they began to become regulars at one of Harlem's famous jazz clubs. They befriended many jazz musicians and popular singers. Their lifestyle was transformed to another level. They were always invited to all the ritzy upscale parties, exclusive dinner functions, and main sporting events. Minnie joined a health spa in Manhattan where she enjoyed long hours of swimming, exercise (although she never stuck to a diet), mud skin treatments and body massages.

Tazi had the pleasure to become best friends with the owner's son at one of their favorite clubs. His name was Lou Workmeister, Jr. Lou was the manager of the club and a body builder who modeled for one of the national health magazines. He was tall, blonde, and Irish—always showing his big white teeth. Each time the Goopoos came to the joint they saw Lou slumped over the bar sipping his favorite drink, Chivas Regal scotch. He would then waddle around the place grinning and offering free drinks on the house without his father's approval. Minnie found Lou Jr. interesting. When he was sober, he was the club's public relations king. He invited the town's best partygoers to the place. Members of the NAACP, novelists, publicists, musicians, Broadway actors and actresses, and black artists became regulars.

Lou and his dad, Lou Sr. lived in Rochester, New York, in a picket-fence neighborhood-style dwelling. On Sundays, Tazi and Minnie became regular dinner guests. They also found out how Lou Sr. had acquired so much flesh. The Workmeisters served heaps of fattening foods. On the table were piles of steak, mashed potatoes (smothered in gravy), pork chops, fried chicken, hog mog and chitterlings, and lots of pastries and pies. Lou Sr. had gained three hundred pounds as a result of this sin. There had been no lesson learned between the two, because three years before, Lou's mother had died of a stroke.

During one Sunday dinner, Lou Jr. told Minnie and Tazi that one of his neighbors had just moved out of the valuable piece of property next door. The Workmeisters were the only white family in this entire neighborhood. He gave the Goopoos the real estate agent's number. The turn-of-the-century Victorian home discovered the next day was a lovely sight to see. The house was very huge. Minnie's first discovery indoors was the masonry fireplace with a mantle of fine wood. The walls were designed with paisley printed paper. Minnie's first words when she stepped inside were, "Oh my gosh, there are so many rooms that you could get lost." There was a living room, dining area, gourmet kitchen, two guest rooms, a den, basement, master bedroom, three bathrooms, and a screened-in back porch. All of the ceilings were well-insulated to protect against the cold, stormy winters. Minnie was thrilled by the back screened-in porch, because she could hear the soothing sounds of a nearby pond. The existing basement was very dark and spooky, so Tazi had their decorator design new windows and walls to bring it alive. Their back yard simply enhanced nature. There was a weeping willow tree, and its leaves crawled all over their eccentric wooden stockade fence. Inside the fence lay a seventy-five square foot Sylvian pool filled with water. In the corner beside it sat a *Petticoat Junction* style hot tub shaped like a round barrel. It was grooved into the ground and was surrounded by philodendron leaves.

Directly across the road lived a black single widow named Hazel. She was too friendly—and simply deceitful. Minnie said that she welcomed them to the neighborhood by baking a blueberry pie. Afterward, she constantly invited herself by the house at any wee hour of the night, wearing exotic nightgowns that showed most of her cleavage and her body-building figure. The Goopoos later learned she had a sister in California who was a plastic surgeon. Her body parts were well proportioned from dozens of surgical enhancements. Minnie giggled as she described some of Hazel's Frederick's of Hollywood lingerie. After a few weeks, Hazel started doing special things for Tazi that led to a secretive affair. Tazi was spellbound by Hazel's body, although he never touched her. She would always leave her bedroom window open, which faced the front of her house, and undress at midnight. Tazi said that she would then climb up and down a door and swing in many positions.

Tony asked Tazi, "Were you guilty about this, Man?"

Tazi simply replied, "I didn't feel guilty at the time, because I loved what I saw."

Tony thought to himself, *This peeping Tom human must have seen something.*

Minnie continued to tell the story by saying, "Every night, Tazi would beg me to go to bed, and as I began to snore, he would rise and run to the window for the upcoming glimpse of *Playboy Live!*"

On one particular night, Minnie awakened to a big surprise. She caught her husband peeking behind her blue satin curtains at Ms. Hazel, who was standing at her window peeling articles of clothing from her silicone body components. Minnie suddenly grabbed a chair and threw it at her cheating husband. Luckily, the chair missed Tazi's head, but it shot straight through the window onto the ground. Minnie began to curse in Spanish, a language she had acquired in high school. She also started tossing Tazi's clothes out of the bedroom window, which had no glass now. Tazi tried to explain his "dirty old man" mentality, but Minnie treated him as if she needed a Miracle Ear hearing aid appointment. She insisted that Tazi leave and never return. After a few months of loneliness and counseling, Minnie decided to reconcile with her problematic husband, after she sashayed over to Hazel's and urged her to stop her *Playboy* and *Hustler* magazine lifestyle.

After returning home, Tazi had a change of heart. He was truly sorry for hurting his wife. Minnie was also. She told us she was partly to blame because she wore lots of flannel and always complained of headaches at bedtime. They both finally put their unused hot tub to use and heated up soft steam every summer night. Minnie laughed as she said, "We felt like steamed vegetables every time we used it." They started taking romantic vacations, because Minnie wanted to travel to Hawaii, Mexico, and the Caribbean. Minnie's favorite yearly retreat was their villa in Palm Springs, California. Every year after the holidays, when it was cold, they would pack their Kinte cloths, luggage, and a travel attitude, and then fly the friendly skies. They loved the West because it represented sunshine and sand. Tazi enjoyed sitting under a palm tree to write and found it provided a natural breeze. Neither swam, but they took long walks across the sand and smiled at the success and the accomplishments in their lives.

During the spring of 1985, Tazi sent airline tickets to Africa for his whole family to visit America for the first time. Pierre, Pierre's wife Thabena, and Tazi's grandparents arrived at La Guardia airport with saucer eyes. Minnie said she was happy to welcome them to America, but their clothes were an instant embarrassment. They were all wearing bright folk costumes–dress wraps accented with beadwork around their dark necks. Thabena's hairstyle was dry and brittle. Minnie said in her mind, *Oh, boy, maybe I'll treat her to a Revlon perm.* Thabena looked like a 1970s Afro-Sheen commercial candidate. Their African printed luggage was made of straw fabric and looked like bags of grain. Tazi's grandmother kept bobbing her head and grinning in silence. She was wearing an Afro-centric headwrap which enhanced her beautiful, radiant, dark skin.

They bore many African presents, such as fruits, fabrics, and recipes from the Motherland. They spoke little English, but they still enjoyed a week of shopping and viewing New York's high-rise buildings, restaurants, and fast-paced lifestyle. Grandfather Goopoo's tobacco habits prevented Minnie from getting close to him. He smoked African cigars and told tales of Africa to everyone he encountered. Minnie laughed as she told us that Grandma Goopoo had given her an African facial using a ground wood product mixed with water and coral which clumped to form a mud pack. After her first application, Minnie vowed to never try this act of skin beauty again. The mud pack dried hard as concrete. She further said that her face felt like a brick as she tried to rinse the wood off after ten minutes. As the rinsing continued, the mud dropped into the sink like pebbles were falling from her face.

Although they got on her nerves, Minnie couldn't resist loving these African folks. They were so down-to-earth and such valuable folks of the world. *It's amazing how people all over the world can come together and share their pride and stories,* Minnie thought. Before the Goopoos left, they blessed Tazi's and Minnie's marriage and told them to continue to strive to stay together in peace and harmony. One special gift Pierre bore was an ivory elephant tusk, which Minnie placed on a statue at her museum.

. . . *Wake up! Wake up Tony!* He had fallen asleep.

What part did I miss?" he blurted. As Minnie smiled at Tony, she simply ended their love story by advising us that keeping magic alive daily, respect, and outweighing problems make a great recipe for a good marriage. She also shared that the ingredients included spontaneity, freedom, sensual exchanges, laughs, and friendship. These things should mix into a large bowl and settle. Additionally, she said they overcame their financial burdens by not depending on each other for money, but by putting what they had together to increase its value.

I was entranced by this intriguing and wonderful story. I learned about what it takes as individuals to come together and share and resolve our problems. We must withstand trials, tribulations, and suffering to make room for our blessings. That's a life to value and trust.

Chapter Seventeen

Dining with the Goopoos

Our dinner was scrumptious. Minnie and Tazi brought along an African dessert that they wanted everyone to try. The dish was called Honeycomb Pie. Tazi said this was his grandmother's favorite recipe. I nibbled on a piece, but found it tasted chalky and unpleasant, like Maalox. *Where was the honey taste?* I thought. The children couldn't hide their thoughts of the taste. Annnabella and Brandon both cringed and held the clump in their mouths without swallowing. I had to allow them to excuse themselves to get rid of the unwanted soggy taste that was held imprisoned in their kiddie taste buds. I apologized for their rude actions, but Tazi accepted it because he said all children had to get used to the taste to appreciate it. On the contrary. *How can he say this, when I'm an adult and despise this recipe like the flu*, I thought. Afterward, the Goopoos decided to stay until we left to go home.

Chapter Eighteen

Pre-ending

It was time for us to head back to Baltimore. It was approximately seven o'clock in the evening and we were walking out of Carol's door. Our goodbyes were sad, but simple. Carol and I arranged to keep in touch via e-mail and telephone. She even said she had purchased some Broadway tickets for Brandon and me to see *The Lion King,* but they were post-dated for September, 1998.

Before we finally left, I went back upstairs and wrote out some postcards for family and friends and made a few phone calls. One call was to my mother Gloria and one was to my best friend Clara Anderson. Clara and I had been friends since the birth of my son. We were inseparable, like Laverne and Shirley. After I placed my call, Clara answered the phone in a sleepy tone. "Hello, is this Denise?"

"Yes, how is it going, Girl?" I said.

"Great, but tell me about New York!"

"Well the trip has been a delight, but I will have to tell you about a serious issue I must deal with when I return home."

"Is it Tony again?"

"Yes, how did you guess?"

"Because before you left for your trip, you felt that he was seeing someone else." As Clara spoke, gurgling sounds cooed through the telephone line from her baby girl, Morgan.

"I didn't want to ruin this trip so I held back from bringing up the issue. I did enjoy the moments of this holiday and Thanksgiving, which is time for prayer and thanks. I also didn't feel like dealing with an unfaithful man," I spurted.

"Did you get to shop?"

"A little, but because there was not much time, I just picked up small souveniers I think everyone will personally enjoy."

After our half-hour conversation ended, I forgot to tell Carol about it. I'm afraid she'll find out when she gets her phone bill, and our friendship will be short-lived. Don't you think that I did the right thing by not telling hr? Maybe not.

Talking to my mother was a joy. She simply shared the interesting things that happened at her dinner table. Her guests included her sisters and brothers. She said all of her turkey vanished within an hour!

"How did this happen?" I asked.

"Well, after everyone finished their meal, they began to pack up a plate."

"They didn't leave any turkey scraps?"

"Nothing but bones," Mother replied.

"Who broke the wishbone this year?"

"Aunt Rue and Joy challenged the dry bone effect."

"So tell me, who won?" I replied.

"Aunt Rue, and now she's making wedding plans without a mate," Mother laughed.

"How did Aunt Joy's face look after she lost?"

"Like she had aged ten years," Mother said.

"Did you have a thrilling time, Denise?"

"Yes Mother, and I will tell you all about it when I get back home," I said. "Mother, for right now, I'll just say, "I LOVE NEW YORK."

"Goodbye dear!" Mother shouted.

"I love you so much," I gladly whispered.

Chapter Nineteen

Closing

We were cruising down by Riverside as the dark clouds descended from the sky. I had finally begun to relax and close my eyes while the truck drifted away from New York. The children seemed like happy campers who had enjoyed this blessed holiday.

Our trip ended after we exited the George Washington Bridge. It began to rain heavily and the temperatures dropped below thirty. This caused the traffic to maneuver in crippled unison.

Stress began to build up in my brain as I peeked at the gas dial, which haunted me. Because it pointed directly to E," I imagined that any minute the truck would stall. *Why would Tony attempt a devastating challenge such as this?* I thought. *My gosh, what a jerk! Now, I guess we will have to depend on one of these hostile Americans to aid us with our gasoline woes.*

My mind was so clouded with anger because as we were loading our luggage in the truck earlier, I had come across a woman's telephone number with lipstick smeared across a grocery bill. I deceitfully placed the unwanted piece of paper into my slacks pocket and kept it until this moment. I suddenly shouted, "Why did you wait until we decided to leave New York to realize that we needed gas?"

"Because there was no time," he uttered.

"That would have been common sense, don't you think?" I replied.

"Why are you so touchy?"

"I have my reasons," I shouted again.

As our heated argument continued, the children played with some of Brandon's action figures. I decided that this would be a good time to exhale.

"Can I ask you a question?"

"Yes," Tony said.

"What is this?" I asked, as I threw the unwanted paper in his lap.

"This is a partner of mine named Maria," Tony muttered.

"Oh really? I think you are lying," I yelled.

"Let's discuss this later Denise, and I am tired of you accusing me of cheating," Tony replied.

"This is not the first number I've ever found on you and probably not the last, you jerk," I shouted.

"What?" he blurted.

"Hello, what part didn't you understand?" I screeched, as tears welled up in my eyes.

"Shut up, Denise," Tony yelled. The rain that was pouring suddenly turned into a light mist.

Silence filled the truck as Tony's anger took control of him and he sped along into a gas station. While he drained a refreshing drink of gas into the bone-dry truck, I ran to the public restroom to dry my tears, but there was no tissue. There were only hard hand towels available. This would only scratch more problems into my life. I decided to walk outside and stand beside a telephone booth. This was where I began to weep. My entire mind was filled with the venomous, shrewd words that Tony and I had just exchanged. While the tears dropped, I peered through them and clearly witnessed an extremely attractive man standing before me. He was very tall, with silky hair and cinnamon skin. He was sort of Spanish-looking, with a head full of silky hair, but I later learned he was half American India and half African-American. As he stood before me like a father protecting his child, he introduced himself as Bhavesh Shah from Silver Springs, Maryland. He suddenly asked, "Are you okay, Dear?" as he pulled out a handkerchief and put it into one of my hands.

"Yes," I spoke softly.

"Is there something that I can do for you?" Bhavesh replied.

"No, thank you, I'll be fine," I sniffed.

Bhavesh was wearing a pair of khaki Chaps shorts and an Indianapolis 500 tee shirt. He also wore a neat pair of Italian leather sandals. He decided to tell me a little about himself before he trotted off. Ironically, we both were from Maryland. I also learned his father lived in the city right around the corner from me. "Wow, isn't this truly fate? Don't you agree?"

Bhavesh was a computer engineer for MCI. He was thirty-five years old and sophisticated. I was amazed by his personality, so we exchanged telephone numbers.

He asked, "May I see you again?"

"Sure," I said.

I didn't feel guilty about what had just occurred because Tony and I had been on the verge of a break-up right before this vacation was planned. I also learned that for the past few months, Tony had been seeing a toy soldier. *What an asshole.* With all the military sexual harassment laws being implemented in Maryland, why was he such a womanizer? *Who cares now,* I thought, *because now I will be seeing an Aladdin look-a-like.*

Bhavesh asked if he could walk me back to the truck, but I explained to him that he couldn't and why. He pointed to his car, which shone like the costume Darth Vader wore in the movie *Star Wars*. It was a 1994 Nissan Maxima, built to perfection. There was a guy in the passenger seat of the car. Bhavesh told me it was his cousin, Dileb, who was visiting from India for the holiday. As the black stainless steel car drove off, Bhavesh waved back with a smile. I wondered where this would go. Right now, I needed a crystal ball, but where would I find a psychic?

I decided to place a call to one of my best friends back home, Mary Nooky. I gleefully told her about my New York discoveries, including just meeting Bhavesh. She was thrilled! I then walked back to the little truck with a new attitude. I had big plans for the future. I smiled at the children and buckled my seat belt with enthusiasm.

As we rambled down the road heading home, I closed my eyes and contemplated how to end this story.

To sum it up, New York had truly been an adventure; all that, and very memorable! It was a place I had only seen in movies, magazines, and on calendars, but now I had been in the picture.

Also, enjoying one's holiday away from home can be gratifying. I guess by now you are planning your New York holiday vacation, but remember to pray about it and then . . . .

Enjoy it in style . . . .